A HEART'S FOREVER HOME

A LOVE'S ROAD HOME NOVEL - BOOK 3

LENA NELSON DOOLEY

To Twila,
Enjoy!
Lena Nelson
Dooley

WILD HEART
BOOKS

ISBN-13: 978-1-942265-36-8

This book is dedicated first to my Lord and Savior Jesus Christ, who has held me close to his heart all my life. I gave my life to Him when I was seven years old. He has been with me through over seven decades, through the best of times and the worst of times. 2021 has had some of the worst of times, but He never left us. My husband and I both contracted Covid 19 in January. My case was mild, and I was well in ten days. James's case was just the opposite. We had literally thousands of people, some from foreign countries, praying for him through the whole time. Even when medical personnel and people in the rehab facility thought he wouldn't live, we never stopped praying. And my husband is now a walking miracle, thanks to the Lord.

And every book I write is dedicated to the love of my life, James, who loved me in 1964 when we married and our love has grown larger for 56 years. He's the best half of our relationship. He's loved me, cherished me, protected me, and provided for me in amazing ways. We've been married so long that it almost hard to remember my life without him. We laugh together, enjoy spending time with each other, and we've been blessed with children, grandchildren, and now eight great-grandchildren. We love spending time with our expanding family, and we love to serve the Lord in any way He desires.

CHAPTER 1

FORT WORTH, TEXAS –APRIL 1896

"*How* dare you?" Anger burst into flames deep inside Theresa Hilliard. She slapped the leering unkempt face of the beastly man.

The smack echoed through the entryway, and her palm stung.

His bloodshot, bleary eyes widened, and he froze in shock for only a moment.

Her brother Quinton hadn't darkened the door of the mansion since his father threw him out for his wastrel ways. Now he was back. The butler had let him in, then gone back to whatever Mrs. Richards had him doing before the loud knocking on the front door.

Quinton caught Theresa when she stepped off the lowest step of the staircase, his hands roving places they shouldn't have as he'd tried to pull her into an unwanted embrace. His voice deepened into a menacing growl. The things he said he wanted to do to her were sickening. Her heart raced like a fast drumbeat in her ears, almost drowning out his muffled words.

After the slap, she whirled to flee back up the staircase. He grabbed at her again, this time catching her sleeve. She pushed against him. In his inebriation, his foot slipped. While he grabbed the banister for balance with his other hand, she pulled away and ran up the steps, leaving the torn sleeve in his hand.

By the time she reached the top, his thunderous exclamations filled the foyer with filthy words and insulting epithets aimed at her. She was glad their younger sisters were in their rooms near the back of the second floor, so they couldn't hear his awful words.

He stumbled up the stairs, unable to catch her.

"You'll regret this, you ingrate." His slurred words and heavy steps came closer.

She reached her room and slammed the door behind her. Using the key, she turned the lock until it clicked and removed it from the keyhole. She stepped away from the door, wrapped her arms across her waist, and tried to stop herself from shaking. But it didn't work.

Once, she had watched Quinton as he slid a piece of paper halfway under a door. Then, poking something in the keyhole from the outside, he worked it against the key until it dropped on the paper, which he pulled under the door—with the key on top. She couldn't risk that happening today. Maybe she should try to wedge a piece of furniture as a barricade against the knob. Her gaze darted around the space. What could she use?

The doorknob turned and he pounded on the door. "Theresa, come out this minute."

"Quinton!" Both of her younger sisters had evidently burst from their separate rooms into the hallway and run toward their brother, meeting him outside her door.

In her mind's eye, she could see them hug him, and she heard every word they said. While she listened, she pulled off her torn dress and donned another one.

"Are you here to stay?" Twelve-year-old Alice's sweet voice sounded hopeful.

"Of course. Since Granny died, I came to claim my inheritance." The sneer in his tone cut through Theresa's heart like the razor-sharp stiletto on display in her father's office.

"Why weren't you at the funeral?" Clara, their sixteen-year-old sister, asked the question Theresa wanted answered.

"No one let me know about her death until today." He sounded so matter-of-fact, blaming others. Just like he always had.

The note of self-righteousness in his voice soured Theresa's stomach.

"How could we? We had no idea where you were." Clara wasn't going to let Quinton off the hook so easily. "I smell alcohol on your breath, and your clothes reek with tobacco smoke. You're even slurring some words. Evidently, you've been doing the same things that caused Father to kick you out of the house in the first place."

He growled deep in his throat. A wild animal sound. At least he wasn't shouting more obscenities. Not right then anyway.

"Just look at you." Clara raised her voice a notch. "How long has it been since you bathed, shaved, and put on clean clothes?"

"You impudent child. I ought to take you over my knee and apply the discipline the old man never did."

"You wouldn't dare!"

"Quinton!" Alice sounded scared. "Why are you acting like this?"

Not wanting Quinton to harm their little sisters, Theresa unlocked the door and stepped into the hallway. "What do you think you're doing? Scaring your little sisters like that."

He turned toward her, a sneer on his face. "So, you're coming out of hiding."

She gave him a hard stare. "Alice, Clara, come downstairs. I'll have breakfast with you today."

Her sisters started toward her.

"Oh no, you don't."

He grabbed each younger girl by the arm. His grip looked extremely tight. The girls would have bruises. "Theresa won't be staying here any longer."

Tears streamed down Alice's cheeks as Clara started pounding him on the chest with her other fist.

"Let go of them, Quinton. You're hurting them." Theresa used her most authoritative tone.

He released his sisters and shoved them away from him as if they were light as a feather, then set his sights on Theresa. "You, start packing a carpetbag. That and your clothes are all you can take. And nothing valuable. All of those things now belong to me."

The gall of the man. He had no claim to anything here. When their parents died, Abuela inherited everything. The lawyer would tell them how the estate would be divided. He'd promised to come later today. She hoped nothing would delay him. No telling what Quinton would do with the many treasures in the mansion. Probably sell them to support his bad habits.

"Clara," Quinton said, "you watch her and make sure she doesn't take anything she shouldn't."

Her sister placed her fists on her waist, arms akimbo. "I will not. She's our sister as much as you're our brother."

"She is not!" He reached into the pocket of his suit jacket and removed some wrinkled papers. "I looked through Father's files and found this. It wasn't signed by our parents, and there is nothing saying it's been filed in court. That proves she never was adopted. She was nothing but a paid companion for Granny. A *servant*."

"She was not a servant. You are just being mean." Clara looked at Theresa, her gaze full of compassion. "Mother, Father,

4

and Grandmother loved Theresa. They'd be appalled by what you're doing."

His eerie cackle filled the hallway. "Don't worry about her. She's just a guttersnipe from New York City. She came here on an orphan train. She knows how to make it out on the streets of a city." He glared at Clara. "Now, do what I told you and do it now."

He turned so quickly he almost fell. Holding onto the wall, he shook his head as if trying to clear something from his brain. What was left of it after all the years he'd abused alcohol. Giving each of them a hard stare, he stumbled toward his room, threw open the door, and entered without closing it behind him. When he lived there, he'd always closed them out.

They heard him stumbling across the room, then a whoosh as he evidently fell across his bed. In less than a minute, loud snores reverberated through the second floor of the mansion, almost as loud as his rant had been.

"Wait here." Theresa left her sisters and went to close the door.

When she returned, Alice was crying, Clara holding her close, comforting her.

"You can't leave, Theresa. *He* can't make you." Clara's voice wasn't as forceful as it had been with Quinton.

Theresa stared at the closed door. "I'm trying to think how to handle this. I don't want him taking his anger out on you two if I stay."

She led the girls downstairs and into the kitchen. The housekeeper glanced at them then kept right on cooking their breakfast.

"Mrs. Richards, we'll eat in here today." Theresa sat at one end of the table where the servants had already eaten. "We want to be where you are."

The housekeeper bustled around, setting the table and

bringing the food. When she turned her gaze toward Theresa, understanding filled her eyes.

Unable to convince herself she would be able to swallow anything she tried to eat, Theresa moved her food from one side of her plate to the other. "When will Mr. and Mrs. Benton return from visiting their daughter and grandchildren? I thought they'd be home by now."

"They should be here today, I think. I don't know what will happen when they return, what with..." Mrs. Richards turned back toward the stove without finishing her sentence.

Their cook and gardener would have a big surprise when they arrived. No telling what Quinton would do to them. Theresa hoped he wouldn't wreak any more havoc after she was gone.

But she would have to leave, because Quinton could take his frustration out on the younger girls if she stayed. Maybe even the servants, but she hoped not. She would miss her sisters and this wonderful woman who had served her and her Abuela so faithfully. A grim future loomed over her. She hadn't seen even a glimpse of her older brother who protected her at school when she first came to the family in that monster upstairs.

Sixteen-year-old Clara took a bite of the fluffy scrambled eggs and swallowed it almost whole. Then she played with what was left on her plate.

"Theresa, you don't have to do what Quinton told you." Clara turned tear-filled eyes toward her. "You belong here more than he does."

"I know, but if those papers *are* the legal ones, he may have the right to throw me out." She put a bit of food in her mouth and felt it turn to sawdust. She washed it down with the milk beside her plate. She couldn't swallow another bite.

Twelve-year-old Alice came around the table and put her arms around her, leaning her sweet head against her shoulder. "Please, Theresa, don't leave. We need you here. We don't know what bad things Quinton might do." She was the age she had been when she became a apart of the Hilliard family.

Theresa's heart broke. How could she leave her sisters? Yet, how could she not? She prayed the lawyer would come today as he said he would. He was the only one who could make sense of what was happening.

"Thank you, Mrs. Richards, for breakfast. I'm going to do what Quinton said."

The cook nodded toward the younger girls and headed out the door. Her "tsk, tsk" followed her, but Theresa knew Mrs. Richards would do whatever she could to protect the younger sisters.

"Alice, you stay here with Mrs. Richards. Maybe you can help her make cookies or a cake." Clara's voice came closer and closer behind Theresa.

"Of course, she can." The woman sounded almost like a grandmother.

At the foot of the stairs, Theresa turned around. "You don't need to help me. I'll follow his directions."

"I'm coming anyway." Clara followed Theresa up the stairs.

How she loved both of these girls. They truly were the sisters she'd never had. And being a member of this family had erased much of the pain she'd experienced when she'd scrounged what she could on the streets of New York City.

The moment Quinton had uttered the word "guttersnipe," memories crept back into her mind, and she couldn't lock them out. The terrible names some people called her because she was Irish. The awful odors of alleyways and garbage began to mask the wonderful aromas that always filled this house. Even though the steam radiators kept the mansion comfortable in this cold weather, the cold from the past seeped toward her bones. What in the world would she do now?

She'd face that when she left the mansion.

Clara caught up with her. "If we're really quiet, maybe Quinton won't wake up until you're finished packing."

"I hope that's true." Theresa eased her bedroom door open.

Her sister followed her inside. "While he's asleep, you can pack whatever you want to take with you."

Theresa pulled her sister into her arms. "I can't do that. If I don't follow his drunken orders, he might hurt you or Alice. I can't risk that." She kissed Clara on the cheek.

After getting the largest carpetbag out of the closet, Theresa opened it on the bed. First, she and Clara folded and placed some of her unmentionables in the bottom. Clara added her two warmest night dresses and robes.

Theresa had a hard time deciding what else to pack. Everything had so much sentimental value. Things Abuela insisted on buying her. Books, jewelry, painting supplies, knickknacks, and much more. She carefully wrapped and added all the bag would hold. A few books, some of the jewelry her grandmother purchased after Quinton was sent away by their father—he wouldn't know it was gone—clothing, two pairs of high-topped shoes and the button hook to close them. They stuffed the bag to nearly overflowing.

She took a long look around the room, and so many things tugged at her heart. She had spent so much of her eight years in this family with their grandmother that she knew more than any of her siblings about family history. About Abuela's grandmother who had been born in Spain. How she had worn that grandmother's wedding dress when she married the grandfather who was gone before she, Traesa, came into the family. Abuela had filled a void in her life. They enjoyed the time they spent together. The nerve of Quinton calling her a paid servant. She had never been that.

Tears built in her eyes, and she tried to keep them from falling. The pain of leaving all the precious mementos clogged her throat with tears. She quickly turned back to her luggage.

Clara peeked out between the draperies. "It looks so cold out there, and a strong wind is bending bare tree limbs almost to the ground. You must wear your warmest clothes."

She helped Theresa put on as many layers as she could. Woolen flannel petticoats topped by two warm skirts and a couple of waists. Then the new coat Abuela had the seamstress create for her not long before she passed away.

Theresa added a velvet hat that covered most of her hair. Fur-lined leather gloves went on last. She felt like a sausage with so many layers on.

Once again, she hugged Clara, whose tears streamed down her cheeks. "I'll always love you, and I'll never forget you. I'll be praying for God to protect you." She stepped back and studied her sister's features, implanting them in her heart and mind. "I'm not going to say good-bye to Alice. It would break her heart…and mine."

Without another word, she headed toward the front door. Thankfully, Quinton hadn't awakened. She couldn't have handled another cruel, terrible altercation.

CHAPTER 2

The day Theresa Kildare's life disintegrated, an unusually late spring freeze blew icy winds toward the Hilliard mansion perched high on a bluff above the Trinity River. She had heard two of the maids talking about it before Quinton arrived. Gale force, the winds whistled across the wraparound porch, up the pitched roof, and down the chimneys, forcing smoke and ashes back inside the grand house. Everything she wore now smelled of the acrid smoke.

The servants valiantly worked to set the dampers in the chimneys to stop the invasion of debris. Theresa didn't envy them that job. Now she had to find a job for herself, and it could be even worse than the ones in this house.

She stopped in the foyer. After buttoning her warmest coat snug around her neck and anchoring her hat with several jeweled hatpins Abuela had given her before she died, Theresa picked up the tapestry carpetbag. What was in the bag was a small percentage of the belongings she'd obtained during the time she lived as a granddaughter in the family.

She added a long wool scarf over the top of her hat and knotted it under her chin. To this she added another heavy scarf wrapped around her neck with the ends hanging in front of her shoulders on either side.

She picked up her carpetbag again and stepped onto the front porch. The wind circled the columns and sliced through all the layers she wore as if they were made of thin silk, raising gooseflesh up and down her body. Even though she had wiped off the tears before she left the house, more dripped down her cheeks.

Yes, she grieved leaving the only home she had known since she was twelve years old. But she grieved the loss of her grandmother even more, the one person she could truly depend on since her parents died. The chill caught her breath, so she pulled the ends of the scarf up over the bottom of her face, anchoring them across her nose with one gloved hand.

When she asked for the coach to be brought around for her ride, she found out that Quinton had dismissed their chauffeur when he arrived home. She had no one to drive her, and the house was on the outskirts of Fort Worth. She'd have to walk quite a ways before she could catch a ride on a streetcar or find a hansom cab. The streetcar would be the cheapest option, so she would have to push forward until she got to this end of the line. She had put a little money in the pocket of her coat. The rest of the paltry sum she'd saved from the spending money her grandmother had given her was hidden at the bottom of her luggage and wouldn't last long. At least the wind would be to her back and not pushing against her.

Theresa didn't feel God's presence with her today. How could she? Surely, the good Lord wouldn't have allowed her erstwhile brother to throw her out like so much garbage. This felt worse than being an orphan on the streets of New York City. At least there, she'd made friends with the other homeless children, and together they'd been able to eke out enough food and scavenge enough clothing to keep fed and warmed.

She must find a job and a place to stay by the time the sun

set that evening. Otherwise, she didn't know what she would do. The only person she knew who might help her was Mr. Wilson Pollard, Abuela's lawyer. He was the only other constant in Theresa's life besides her grandmother. Well, he and the pastor of Abuela's church.

But the Reverend had moved to a town in Indiana just last week to pastor a church near his wife's family. And the new pastor hadn't been by the house to visit with Grandmother before she died. Theresa did see him at the funeral, but only in passing. Of course, with him just coming to the new pastorate, he was probably too busy to visit all the shut-ins before Abuela was gone.

The longer Theresa walked, the colder she became. Shivers ran up and down her spine. She pulled the scarf tighter over her face.

Her toe caught on something. Her knees buckled, and she couldn't keep her balance. With a very unladylike thump, she landed on the icy roadway. She glanced around to see if anyone was looking, but the street was deserted. The smart people stayed inside on days like that one.

Tears streamed down her cheeks. She rested a moment, but the chill from the ground steeped through the layers. Between the wool petticoats, the multiple skirts, and her aching ankle, it took two tries to get to her feet.

She would probably be bruised and sore tomorrow. Maybe the long walk would work out some of the soreness. She trudged until her feet and hands began to numb.

Theresa glanced up. She had almost reached the end of the streetcar line. One of the cars was stopped and taking on passengers, and she was close enough to reach it before it left. The first good thing that had happened to her that day. She prayed it wouldn't be the last.

$\sim$

*W*ilson Pollard hunched over his desk, going over the contract he'd written for one of his clients, making sure he'd included every detail the client requested.

After he finished, he stood and stretched. "Aaaaah."

Even though twenty-five didn't make him an old man, if he spent too long sitting and working on papers, his back got tired. He reached his arms toward the ceiling, then down to touch his toes before standing erect again. Twisting his upper body from side to side helped release the tension gripping his muscles.

He needed to go for a walk and stretch his legs. Just as that thought flitted through his mind, the front doors rattled from the force of the winds. *Maybe the walk will have to wait.* Soon, it would be time for him to eat lunch. He dreaded going out in the icy wind to his boardinghouse. He should have brought his lunch. Maybe he should buy some crackers and cheese or potted meat to keep in his desk for times like this.

He was resuming his seat when the front door opened. The wind whipped around a petite figure carrying a rather large carpetbag. She dropped it to the floor with a thump and pushed the door with both hands, trying to shut it against the cold. The wind was winning the battle. He had to bite his tongue to keep from laughing.

Hurrying forward, he helped her push the door closed, glancing down just as she looked up.

"Miss Hilliard, what are you doing here? I have an appointment with your family to read the will this afternoon. You shouldn't have gotten out in this terrible weather."

Her eyes widened then glanced toward the luggage at her feet.

Wilson gulped. Had he made some *faux pas*? Was she going somewhere he hadn't heard about? Planning to invite the Hilliard driver in out of the weather, he looked out the window, searching for the coach. *Nothing.* Surely someone from the house had provided her with a ride downtown.

Something isn't right.

Miss Hilliard sat and huddled in the most comfortable wingback chair beside his desk. She appeared to be bundled in several layers of clothing. Her tightly clasped hands gripped her reticule in her lap, and the carpetbag sagged next to her feet.

He moved close to the desk and waited a moment for her to say something. She didn't even look at him. Her gaze roamed the furnishings and bookcases.

"What can I do for you, Miss Hilliard?"

Her head shot up, and she stared into his eyes. "That's not my name." The words had such a hard edge to them that they dropped like stones between them.

"Theresa, what are you talking about?" He rounded his desk and sat. He didn't want to tower over her.

She stiffened. "And my name's not Theresa either. It's *Traesa Kildare*, a good Irish name, and I'm proud of it." Her chin raised in defiance.

He took a note pad out of his desk drawer. "I'll make a note of that."

She watched his hand as he wrote *Traysa* Kildare on the paper.

"It's T-r-a-e-s-a." Evidently she could read upside down.

He marked a line through what he'd written and copied down the letters she gave him. "I'm confused. I know you were adopted. Mr. Harrison took care of it. Before he retired, he told me you were adopted from the orphan train several years ago." He rested his elbows on the desk and steepled his fingers, tapping the tips against each other.

Traesa took a deep breath, and a few more tears slipped down her cheeks. "Quinton sent me away, saying I was never adopted. He said he had proof." She pulled a hanky from her sleeve and dabbed at her wet cheeks. "I need a job, Mr. Pollard. I was hoping you could help me find one. Maybe I could work for you."

Her tone was so hopeful, and he hated to turn her down, but that could never happen. It wouldn't do for her or for him.

Society would be appalled.

～

*T*raesa watched a myriad of emotions wash across his expressive face. For a moment, she wondered if he was also a trial lawyer. If so, he'd have a hard time keeping people in the courtroom from knowing exactly what he was thinking. And things weren't looking good for her right now. *He is going to turn me down.*

Her stomach, which had felt unsettled already, began to churn. If she'd been home, uh...at the Hilliard mansion, she would have gone to the water closet and lost all her meager breakfast. She covered her lips with her fingers. If she didn't get it to settle down, she would ruin most of the clothing she owned as well as the room-sized rug in this beautiful office. She gritted her teeth, trying to keep her emotions in check, as well as the contents of her stomach.

The handsome man across the desk from her cleared his throat. "I'm afraid, Ther...Traesa, that would be most improper —a bachelor and a beautiful young woman working alone together in an office."

She hadn't thought of that. She didn't care about what was proper in society anymore. Her brother, who was part of Fort Worth society, treated her improperly. No matter what people thought about her, she wanted to work for this man, the only one who had treated her with any dignity since her father died. But she didn't want to damage Mr. Pollard's good name.

His other words finally penetrated her brain.

Beautiful?

The only person who'd called her beautiful since her mother died all those years ago was Abuela. Even though Mr. Pollard probably didn't mean them, the word was like manna to her heart and brought a blush to her face. She felt the warmth as it crept upward.

The lights from the electric wall sconces glistened as tears started to fill her eyes again. She didn't want him to see them, but she knew they would soon start to run down her cheeks. She pressed her hanky against her eyes.

Mr. Pollard stared at her with compassion, which spread across his whole expression. That only caused more tears.

He came around the desk and sat on the front corner, leaning toward her. "I'm so sorry. I didn't mean to make you cry. Do you have any other ideas about what you can do now?"

Surely he knew she wouldn't have sought him out if she had another place to go. Her hands trembled as she shook her head. The only other option would be to become a servant in one of the other cattle-baron mansions, but it was far too cold to go from door to door asking for a position. Of course, she'd heard about the jobs available in the part of town she'd never entered. She'd rather die than go to one of those establishments.

"Miss Kildare, it's time for me to go to lunch. Would you join me? We can eat at the boardinghouse where I live. And we may be able to find a place where you can spend the night in comfort while we try to solve your dilemma."

His words were so kind, how could she refuse?

Mr. Pollard used his telephone to call for a hansom cab to pick them up, and it arrived just moments later. He bundled her up in a blanket and hurried her into the conveyance. The driver had heated bricks waiting at their feet, and he added another blanket for each of them. The ride to the boardinghouse was much more comfortable than her trip from the Hilliard mansion had been.

She huddled in the warm covers thinking about the confident young woman she'd been the last time Mr. Pollard had come to the mansion. She and Abuela had been laughing when he'd stepped into the parlor. Laughing about some foolishness she couldn't even remember now. How had her life so fallen apart? No wonder Mr. Hillard couldn't think of a thing to say. The situation left her speechless as well.

After several minutes, Mr. Pollard cleared his throat. "Twin sisters lived next door to each other, and when both of their husbands died, they decided to open boardinghouses. Their homes are quite large. Mary Kelley runs a boardinghouse for women, and Pat Crawford runs one for men. They work together to cook for both houses, and their food is so delicious, many people who work nearby eat their noon meals there. There'll be plenty for you, too."

Traesa glanced up at him. "That would be nice."

Although she wasn't sure she could eat anything. She was hungry. Maybe her stomach would settle down by the time they arrived.

"I'll use estate money to pay for your meal and for you to stay in Miss Mary's house. When I'm out at the mansion this afternoon, I'll try to get to the bottom of this mess. We can decide what to do tomorrow." His warm smile helped take away some of the chill that had covered her heart the moment Quinton stepped into the house that morning.

It hadn't entered her mind that she probably didn't have enough money to pay for a night at the boardinghouse until the lawyer mentioned using estate money. If Quinton ever found out about it, he would be enraged, but she couldn't think about that right now.

"Thank you, Mr. Pollard."

Traesa's eyes darted from side to side when the cab entered a neighborhood with a wide thoroughfare lined with large trees. Branches formed an arch across the cobbled road. Houses nestled under the protection of the budding trees. Although on this frigid day, the houses didn't need the shade that would soon form. In the hot Texas summer, the canopy would be welcomed. The houses weren't as grand as the Hilliard mansion, and none of them was built of brick, as all the Cattle Baron homes on the bluff were. Still, they were attractive. Fancy scrolled decorations made the clapboard houses look like fancy wedding cakes.

Not that she'd ever seen one of those cakes. Her older sister, who'd married a few years before, had had one, but Abuela hadn't been up to attending the wedding, so Traesa had sat beside her and read to her from her favorite book, the Holy Bible. Her sister's lady's maid described all the details of Charlotte's wedding for Traesa when they all arrived back at the house.

She'd read about such weddings in the novels she enjoyed. Books her grandmother bought for her, but Quinton claimed that the things Abuela bought her belonged to the estate. None of her siblings had read any of them, except Charlotte before she moved to England. Clara and Alice were too busy involved in society functions she'd never attended. Once again, Traesa blinked, trying to keep the tears from making tracks down her cheeks.

The thoughts of weddings brought a sharp pain to her heart. She'd not only lost her younger sisters, she'd never see Charlotte again. She and her duke had come back from England after their first child was born. Holding the sweet baby close, Traesa had dreamed of the time when she would snuggle a baby of her own. Now that might never happen. She'd lost so much in one fell swoop. Her grandmother, all three of her sisters, her fine home, and the servants who were more like family.

The cab stopped in front of a house painted in shades of pink, blue, and lavender, surrounded by yards that were well-manicured, even on this blustery day. A twin to the house, but in darker shades of the same colors, nestled beside the first.

Both looked inviting, not stodgy like the house she'd left this morning had been.

A long room with walls lined with windows connected the two in what was obviously the dining area. Traesa liked the way the tables and chairs were set up with tablecloths and dishes, as if waiting for special guests. Many of them had people smiling, laughing, some already eating.

She needed to feel welcomed and valued, not cast away and worthless. She shook that thought from her head as Mr. Pollard helped her descend from the cab.

When they entered the foyer of the boardinghouse for women, they were met by an atmosphere of comfort and welcome. A young blonde came from the doorway leading to the dining room Traesa had glimpsed before.

"Mr. Pollard, how can I help you?" A wide smile spread across the lady's face.

"I've brought Miss Kildare to stay a while with you, Bridgett." He glanced toward the dining room. "And we're going to have dinner with you. Is Mary around? I'd like to introduce her to Traesa."

Before Bridgett could turn, a woman dressed in the height of fashion emerged behind her. Her shirtwaist had puffy sleeves trimmed in lace at the cuff. Matching lace lined the high neckline. The soft pink blended with the bell skirt made of plaid of rose, black, and white. Traesa felt drawn to the lovely woman.

"Wilson, so good to see you, but aren't you in the wrong boardinghouse?" Her musical laugh accompanied the words.

"I hope I'm not wrong about you having a vacancy. We need a room for Miss Kildare while I'm straightening out her living situation."

Traesa was glad he didn't go into the details of what was happening in her life.

Mrs. Kelley held out a hand. Traesa shook it. "Of course, we'll be glad to have you as long as you need a place to stay."

Those words lifted a heavy burden from Traesa.

Mrs. Kelley turned to Bridgett. "Make up the room on the north corner of the second floor. Mr. Pollard and Miss Kildare will be my guests for dinner. You should have the room ready by the time they're finished." She picked up the carpetbag and gave it to Bridgett.

The young woman led the way a short distance down the hallway to a cloak room. "You can put your outer garments in the closet here. No one will bother them. We'll wait for you in the parlor."

When Traesa opened the closet door, she found several empty wooden clothes hangers on hooks along the back wall. She took the time to remove the extra clothing she'd donned before she left the Hilliard mansion. The room also contained a cheval mirror standing in one corner, so she was able to straighten both her dress and her hair before she joined the others.

Finally, things sounded hopeful.

CHAPTER 3

ilson chatted with Mary Kelley as they waited for Traesa to return, but he was distracted as he looked toward where his client had disappeared. When she reentered the foyer, his eyes widened. The lovely dark green suit mirrored the color of her eyes. She was far from the pitiful-looking woman who'd invaded his office that morning. Head held high, she walked with poise and grace. But as she approached, he caught glimpses of the hurt he'd seen earlier in her eyes. He'd never felt drawn to a woman as much as he did to her.

"Miss Kildare, welcome." Mary's smile drew a corresponding one from Traesa. "Let's get some hot food for both of you. The cold wind slices right through you, doesn't it?"

"Yes, ma'am, like a knife. I'm still almost frozen." Traesa's melodic voice struck a chord inside him.

"Follow me. I have just the thing to take care of that." Mary headed toward an empty table near the fireplace. Roaring flames supplemented the heat from potbelly stoves in the other three corners.

Wilson walked close to Traesa, trying to keep prying eyes

from noticing how her hands shook. Soon after they were seated in the cozy corner, a waitress arrived with mugs of piping hot coffee.

"Thank you, Molly." He smiled up at her.

"I can bring you cocoa instead, if you'd rather." The woman set a cup in front of each of them.

Wilson shot Traesa a questioning glance.

A gentle smile curved her lips while her fingers wrapped around the steaming beverage. "This is just fine with me." She lifted the mug and took a quick sip.

"What can I get you to eat, Mr. Pollard?" Molly took a pencil and a small pad from the pocket of her apron.

"I forgot to look at the posted sign with the choices." He gave the older woman a rueful smile.

"We have a pork roast with carrots and baked apples, and because of the cold weather, we're also offering a hearty beef stew and cornbread. Hot rolls come with the pork."

He turned toward Traesa. "Which would you prefer?"

She gave a tremulous smile to Molly. "The stew and cornbread sound wonderful. It might warm me up quicker."

Wilson nodded. "I'll have the same."

"Right away." Molly's cheery answer trailed her as she headed across the large dining room toward the kitchen.

Conversations at many tables caused a low murmuring. The aromas wafting through the room made his stomach growl. He hoped his companion hadn't heard it.

He reached across the table and felt Traesa's hand. "Are you warming up at all?"

With the other one, she took another sip of the coffee. "This is helping some. As is the fire. I'm sure the food will finish the job." She glanced around the crowded dining room almost as if she didn't want to look straight at him. "You weren't joking when you said this is a popular place to eat. How many of these people live in one of the boardinghouses?"

There were as many people that he didn't recognize as those he did. "It looks to me as if at least half these people aren't from the boardinghouses."

"I suppose this is a good place to meet people from this area of Fort Worth."

Just as Traesa finished that statement, Molly headed straight toward them carrying their food. She set the tray on one side of the table and placed a steaming bowl of stew in front of each of them and a heaping plate with cornbread between them. She added a smaller bowl of butter.

"Thank you." Traesa looked at the food with eager anticipation. "It all smells delicious."

Molly nodded and headed toward the kitchen with her empty tray, stopping along the way to greet some of the regulars.

Wilson stared at Traesa. "Why didn't you eat much breakfast?"

Before she answered, she pressed her lips tightly together and frowned. "The hullabaloo with Quinton stole my appetite."

He looked back toward Traesa. "I'm sorry I said anything. I didn't mean to remind you of what happened."

He sipped his soup and studied Traesa across the table. She'd dug into the stew like a starving woman, and he was glad to see it. Her morning had to have been extremely traumatic. The gall of her brother, throwing her out like that. What would their parents have thought, were they still alive? And older Mrs. Hilliard? She loved Traesa so much. She would be mortified, but then they were all embarrassed about Quinton's behavior. Not like Traesa, who'd never been anything but kind and gentle.

After they'd each eaten a few bites, he put his spoon in his bowl. "How are you doing, really?"

"It's all right. I'm better now." After slicing a piece of cornbread in two, she smeared both halves with butter that quickly melted. A smile crept across her face again as she took a bite. "This is so delicious."

That slight smile pulled at him. But if she could ignore what happened, so could he...for now. While they finished their meals, they chatted, getting to know each other a little better. Traesa was an interesting woman. They shared a love of reading.

When they were finished, he escorted her into the foyer of the women's boardinghouse. "You get settled while I'm gone. I'll go to the mansion and try to set things straight." *If I can.*

In the hansom cab on the way back to his office, he reviewed what he needed to take with him. He couldn't let the Hilliard siblings find out that he knew where Traesa was and what had transpired that morning.

At his office, he asked the driver to wait and hurried inside. He chose several papers to take with him, but not the actual will, and returned to the cab.

The vehicle made the slow ascent up the icy roadway to the mansion while Wilson planned how he would proceed.

When they arrived, he instructed the driver to go around to the back of the house and come in through the servant's entrance. He told the man to tell Mrs. Benton, the cook, that he'd brought the lawyer and ask if he could have some coffee and a warm place to wait. Even though it was unseasonably cold, at least the strong wind of the morning had died down. Knowing Texas, tomorrow could feel like spring.

Clara Hilliard answered the door and invited him in. "Mr. Pollard, we were expecting you. My brother Quinton has come home." A frown puckered her forehead. "I'll let him know you're here. He claims he's the heir to the fortune and the mansion."

"Really? He hasn't been living here for several years, has he?" He hung his hat on the hall tree, then removed his heavy coat and placed it on another branch. *I wonder where Smythe is.* "I'll wait in the parlor, if that's all right?"

"Yes...yes." Clara backed into the hallway and headed up the staircase.

Wilson glanced around the familiar room to see if anything was missing yet. Evidently, the servants were carrying on their good work just as they had while Mrs. Hilliard was alive. The room was spotless, every ornament and knickknack in its usual place. At least, Quinton hadn't started making too many changes. Hopefully, he had the sense to realize that, even if he was the heir, he couldn't claim anything until the will was read.

Quick footsteps down the stairs echoed in the entry hall. When Quinton entered the parlor, Wilson turned to face him.

A wide smile broke across the disheveled man's face as he advanced with one hand held out. "Mr. Pollard, right?"

Wilson gave him a hard stare and ignored the outstretched hand. "And you are?"

The younger man took a step back and wiped his palm on his wrinkled waistcoat. "I'm Quinton Hilliard. The heir."

What arrogance! He needs to be removed from the pedestal he imagines himself on. "Is that so?" Wilson wanted to keep the upstart unsettled. "I don't recall your name being mentioned any of the times I've come here on legal business for Mrs. Hilliard."

Bright red suffused the younger man's cheeks. "I...I've been...away for quite a while. When did you become Granny's lawyer?"

His haughty tone grated on Wilson's nerves. "Several years ago. I was part of her other lawyer's firm, and he assigned the Hilliard estate to me." That should've wiped the snooty expression from the younger man's face, but it didn't.

"And now you're here to read the will?" A hard eagerness suffused his tone.

"Only if everyone mentioned in it is present." Wilson made his tone deadly serious.

The confusion that covered Quinton's face would have been

comical if things hadn't been so serious. "I'm not sure I know what you mean."

"Call everyone who is working here to come to the parlor, and we can get started."

The young man huffed out of the room.

Wilson sat in a wingback chair by the fireplace, welcoming the cozy warmth. While he waited, he considered his strategy.

After a few minutes, Quinton returned, his sisters trailing him.

Mrs. Richards soon arrived, accompanied by three maids.

There should be several others...the butler, the carriage driver and the hostler who shared the work in the stable, the cook, and the gardener. They'd been there the last time he visited Mrs. Hilliard. Had Quinton gotten rid of all of them since he threw Traesa out that morning? If he did, he'd had no right.

Quinton had been pacing the room. When the servants stopped assembling, he stepped in front of Wilson. His scowling frown didn't bode well for the coming conversation. "What are we waiting for? Let's get on with this."

Wilson stood, looming over the younger man. Let the whippersnapper feel the power he held. "I'm sorry. Some of the people mentioned in the will aren't here. I can't read it until they're present."

Dangerous rage shot from Quinton's eyes. "Not read the will?" His tone rose with each word. "You must read it today!" He stopped, took a deep breath, then sealed his lips in a tight line. His face took on the color of beetroot, looking as if he were ready to explode.

Wilson hoped he wouldn't die of apoplexy right here in front of his sisters and the others.

"I'm sorry, Quinton." He needed to calm the man down a little. He took his seat in the chair again. "I'm following the letter of the law. Everyone mentioned in the will must be present."

He didn't say anything else. He just waited to see if Quinton would settle down.

The man stood unflinching for a minute or two before he deflated like a rubber balloon. "Who else is in it?" His arrogance dissipated slightly.

Wilson picked up one of the papers in his lap and started to read. "Your sister, Theresa, of course. Smythe, the butler. Mr. Richards, the carriage driver and grounds keeper. Henry O'Neal, the hostler. George Benton, the gardener and Mrs. Benton, the cook. Mrs. Richards, the housekeeper."

At each name, Quinton flinched. "May I speak to you alone?"

Wilson nodded and stood. He turned his attention toward the others. "I'm sorry for interfering with what you were doing. We won't be reading the will today. I'll return when we have this all worked out."

Quinton watched them until they were out of sight.

Wilson sat back in the chair. "Have a seat, Quinton." He waved him toward the matching chair across the fireplace. "What's going on?"

"I came back because my grandmother died. I'm sure I'm the heir to the fortune, and I need it *right now*." At least, he wasn't as obnoxious as he had been before, but his emphasis told Wilson a lot.

"Where are all these people?" He lifted the paper with the names, then stared at Quinton. Something had to be wrong to make him so desperate.

"I sent Theresa away." Quinton reached into his pocket and removed some folded pages. "She was never adopted."

"According to my dealings with your grandmother, she certainly was."

Quinton held out the papers, and Wilson took them. He read the whole document. "These are valid adoption papers."

"But as you can see, my parents never signed them."

He was right, though there had to be some explanation. "I'll check on this. I'll look through the files in the office from eight years ago and see what we have. There are crates and crates of old documents I'm still going through. I'll get back to you on this as soon as I can find what we need."

"If that's not enough..." Quinton reached into another pocket. "I also have this copy of Granny's will."

Quinton handed another crumpled paper to Wilson. As he glanced through the several pages, anger built inside him. Mrs. Hilliard hadn't written this drivel. It wasn't the phrasing she would have used, nor was that her signature. He'd seen the real one often enough. While he placed these papers with the others he'd brought with him, he took several deep breaths. Now wasn't the time to lose his temper. He needed to wait until he had the proof of whatever laws the despicable man might have broken.

"Now, what about these other people?" He cocked one brow to keep from alarming Quinton the way he wanted to.

"I let them go to save money." The younger man stared straight into his eyes. "I needed to use some of the household money to pay a debt."

This was worse than Wilson had realized. "I'm sorry, but you don't have the authority to fire or hire anyone. Neither do you have the authority to take money from the household account. Until I read the will with everyone present, you don't have any authority whatsoever. I could have you arrested for stealing right now. How did you get the money?"

"Mrs. Richards was kind enough to obtain it for me."

I'm sure he didn't give her any choice. He'd have to talk to her without Quinton around so he could find out exactly what happened. Wilson understood that Quinton's father had disowned the young man until he straightened up, which never happened. No telling how many debts he'd accumulated. The sum must be high, considering how anxious he was to get his hands on cash. Wilson decided to change the estate account so no one but him could withdraw funds since he was the executor.

He gave Quinton a stern stare. "It's your job to find all the people you fired and reinstate them into the household. Understood?"

Red traveled into the younger man's cheeks once again, and his scowl could curdle milk. "Understood." His tone was filled with anger.

Quinton rose from his chair and stalked toward the front window to glance out. He jerked the draperies closed and turned back.

Agitated, he stopped beside Wilson. "You *must* read the will tomorrow then! I'll send word to the others so they'll be here."

With these words, he stomped out into the hallway and up the stairs.

Even though the grandson showed him legal adoption papers that hadn't been signed or filed, he still wanted to make sure Quinton wasn't putting anything over on Traesa. All Mrs. Hilliard's papers included her in the inheritance.

But what if Quinton was right? If the papers hadn't been signed or filed, then Traesa could have been just a paid companion. And what about that will Quinton had produced? Wilson knew it was a forgery. Evidently, Quinton hadn't changed his ways, and he might be in actual danger from someone to whom he owed money. By the looks of him, he had been hanging out with nefarious characters. Wilson wondered what he'd seen when he looked into the street.

So far Quinton had committed two crimes that Wilson knew about, taking money from the estate funds and forging the will. What else had he done?

He didn't know a lot about the baser things in Fort Worth, but he did know there were plenty of dishonest people with illegal businesses. Before he came back to see this family, he'd put out feelers to learn more about Quinton, his associates, and their enterprises. He didn't have hope that he'd find anything good. He wasn't looking forward to digging into that part of the city.

But he must if he was to protect Traesa and her sisters.

CHAPTER 4

*H*oping to find Mrs. Richards, Wilson headed toward her small office at the back of the first floor. As he passed each room, he glanced in to see if it looked as if anything had been removed. So far, nothing. *That's good.*

He stopped outside the housekeeper's office and tapped on the door facing. She lifted her eyes from the ledger open in front of her.

"Come in, Mr. Pollard. How can I help you?" Strain revealed itself in her pinched lips and the lack of sparkle in her eyes.

"I need to talk to you about a serious matter."

She nodded toward the wingback chair across the desk from her. "Please, have a seat."

"I'm trying to get all this inheritance mess straightened out." He dropped into the cushy seat. "Quinton told me you helped him obtain some money from the bank."

Worry puckered her brows, and she hesitated a moment before answering. "Yes."

The word was almost too quiet to hear. Wilson hoped she didn't think he held her responsible.

"I'm not here to reprimand you." He leaned back and relaxed, hoping she would too. "May I close the door? I'd rather no one else hears our discussion, but I'll leave it open if it will make you more comfortable."

She shook her head. "Mr. Pollard, I know you're a man of honor. Go ahead."

After pushing the door closed, he sat back down and studied her for a moment.

"I'm sorry for what I did. I knew it was wrong." She clasped her hands tightly and dropped them on the ledger. Her knuckles blanched almost white.

Whatever Wilson said next had to be something that would help her relax. This was a good woman who had run the household with honesty and integrity as long as he had been the family's lawyer. She'd been there years before that.

"I'm sure you were surprised when Quinton asked you to help him. And I know you didn't want to do what he asked."

She relaxed her hands a little. "I was shocked. I would have never done what he wanted, but he didn't ask." She paused and took a deep breath. "He ordered me. I was about to tell him what I thought about it when his eyes glazed over. He almost looked crazy. Dangerous. That's when he threatened to hurt the younger girls. He'd already sent Miss Theresa away. I had to protect the little ones." A tear slid down one cheek, and she swiped it away. "I love those girls as if they were the children Mr. Richards and I never had."

How dare that man prey on these innocent people, his own sisters?

"I'm here to talk to you about a plan I have to keep anything like that from happening again."

A flicker of hope sparked in her eyes. "If you can do that, I'll be so relieved. I'm just the housekeeper, and now..."

When her voice trailed off, he leaned forward with his forearms on his thighs. "Just relax, Mrs. Richards. Would you to tell me exactly what happened earlier today, with as many details as you can remember? I need to know what we are up against."

He hoped she realized how important it was for him to truly know every detail.

She nodded and relaxed her hands on the ledger. "Mr. Quinton came home. You know that. Things were awful when he did. He was drunk and disorderly. I think that's what you call it. He shouted a lot at Theresa, and his words were cruel, the kind of words that had never been spoken in this house before. I think you know what kind I mean."

He nodded. "I imagine I do. I don't hear them often myself."

An expression of relief spread over her solemn face. "I heard the commotion and hurried toward the front of the house. I'd barely gotten close enough to see them when she started up the stairs. I was horrified when he accosted her. It was as though he were insane. The very idea of him laying his hands on his sister as if she were a trollop made my blood boil, but I knew he wouldn't listen to me."

Her breaths were coming in quick spurts. "I didn't know if I could stop him. He's so much larger than I am, but I was willing to try. Then he stumbled, and she got away, running upstairs as fast as she could, but he was clutching her dress so tight, the sleeve tore off as she ran away."

No wonder Traesa was so upset. If the man had been here right now, Wilson probably couldn't have stopped himself from beating him to a pulp. He knew that Quinton's parents had taught him to be better than that. He had to be involved with some truly terrible people.

"He followed, but he was too drunk to make much headway. She was able to get to her room and lock the door before he got there."

At a pause, Wilson scooted back in the chair, thankful Traesa had been fast enough. If she hadn't… He didn't want to let the consequences into his mind, but they were hard to shove away. "What happened next?"

"The younger girls came from their rooms. They were excited at first. They hadn't seen him in a long while, and I don't think they ever knew why their father sent him away. Theresa came out, probably to make sure he didn't hurt her sisters. But he wasn't interested in doing anything to them. The full strength of his anger was aimed at her."

Wilson had to grit his teeth to keep from saying what he thought about the man. He shouldn't use those words around a lady.

"He told her she wasn't adopted. That he had proof. And he told her to pack only what she could carry in one carpetbag and leave immediately." By now, tears streamed down Mrs. Richards's face. "He told her not to take any of the valuables Mrs. Hilliard bought for her. She'd roll over in her grave if she knew what he said. And his actions were even worse. Poor Theresa must be heartbroken. I wish I knew where she went."

Wilson seethed inside. Maybe it was a good thing Quinton had left when he did. "What did he do then?"

"I heard him stumble to his room. I think he passed out on his bed, because everything got quiet up there."

This poor woman who loved and cared for the family was grieving. Somehow he had to give her some hope.

"What happened next?" He hated to keep pushing her, but he needed all the details.

"Theresa brought Clara and Alice downstairs to eat breakfast. Since the cook and her husband were on a trip, I'd been cooking. This morning, none of those sweet girls ate enough to feed a bird. Then Clara accompanied Theresa to help her pack. Alice and I made cookies to take her mind off what was happening. When we were finished, Theresa was gone." Looking as if she had lost one of her own children, Mrs. Richards slumped before removing a hanky from her sleeve and wiping her eyes.

He sat silently until she pulled herself together. Quinton Hilliard was like a hurricane, leaving unimaginable pain and loss behind him. The man should be tarred and feathered, and right now Wilson would cheerfully volunteer for the task.

"Mr. Pollard, forgive my manners." The housekeeper arose and came around the desk. "I haven't offered you any refreshment. Would you like a pot of tea or some coffee? I'm sure we have a lot more to talk about."

"Thank you. Whichever is easier to fix. We probably will need something to drink while we finish our conversation." He watched her walk out the door. "Oh, wait a minute."

She turned back to look at him. "Yes."

"Where's my driver? I told him to ask Mrs. Benton for something hot to drink and a warm place to wait."

"I'd almost forgotten about him. I gave him the last of the coffee and a couple of cookies. He went out to make sure his horse was all right. I think he took the animal into the stable and stayed out of the weather with him." A frown settled on her face. "I guess I should have checked on him."

"You had enough on your mind. I'll check on him while you fix us something."

He followed her out of the room and headed toward the front of the house to get his coat.

He found the driver talking to his horse. "Are you all right out here?"

The man turned toward him. "Yes. I stayed here when I heard all the shouting and saw the crazy man hurtle out of the house. I didn't want him to take his anger out on me."

"Right. I won't be much longer."

Returning to the house, he walked all around the lower floor while the housekeeper was fixing the drinks. He knew there was a safe in Mr. Hilliard's study, so he stepped inside to search for it. When he found the heavy steel door behind a section of the bookcases, he tried to open it. It wouldn't budge. Maybe

Quinton hadn't been able to open it either. He had, however, gone through the drawers in the desk. Every one of them was a mishmash of papers and other items in haphazard order.

Wilson was pretty sure there hadn't been any money there. Mrs. Hilliard was not in the habit of leaving cash around the house. If Quinton owed money to the wrong kind of people, he was desperate to get his hands on ready cash. No wonder he was frantic. Wilson sensed that everyone in the house was in danger if Quinton returned. When Wilson got back to his office, he planned to hire a couple of men to guard the place. He couldn't take a chance of him doing more harm to anyone who lived there.

He headed back to Mrs. Higgin's office just in time to see her set a tea tray on a table in front of the settee along the wall by the door.

She stood straight and turned toward him. "I brought the cookies Alice and I made this morning." She gestured for him to sit on the settee, and she pulled a nearby chair to the other side of the table.

"Thank you. Both the tea and the cookies will really hit the spot." He reached for one of the snickerdoodles, his favorite. "Where are the girls now?"

"After Quinton ran out, they went back upstairs. I'm sure they're talking about what happened. Clara will be comforting Alice and taking care of her. It's been a hard day for everyone." The housekeeper poured two cups of the tea. "Would you like lemon, milk, or sugar in your tea? I even brought some honey if you like that better."

"Just a touch of honey will be fine."

The steaming brew warmed him some when he took a sip. He set his cup back down.

"Let's get back to your story."

"The Bentons arrived, and Quinton staggered downstairs, still in his rumpled clothes. When he reached the bottom, he fired Mr. Smythe on the spot. My husband came inside about that time, and Quinton fired him too. Then he turned to me and told me I could stay. He needed someone to cook. My dear husband and I stared at each other. After all the years we've been married, he knew I wouldn't leave the girls. He gave a slight nod to me before he went to pack." She stopped and took a drink and nibbled on a cookie.

"So he fired everyone else. The Bentons and Mr. O'Neal, too?"

Quinton needed to be taken off the streets. Maybe Wilson should bring charges against him for taking the money and forging the will. He'd consider that when the young man came back.

If he came back.

"That's exactly what he did. He threatened to sell all the horses and the carriage, but he didn't have time to before you came." Mrs. Richards looked as if she had shriveled up while they were talking. She was carrying so much sorrow and responsibility.

"Here's my plan. As soon as I get back to my office, I'll be hiring a few men, so you'll have guards around the clock. They'll remain hidden unless Quinton shows up."

She let out a long sigh. "I'm glad to hear that."

"I'll draw up legal papers naming you the guardian for Alice and Clara. That way you'll have the authority you need to take care of them. I'll change the paperwork at the bank, so I'll be the only person who can draw money out of the estate account. Don't worry. I'll make sure you have all the funds you need, and you can contact me if you need extra. That way, Quinton can't force you to get more money for him. Of course, the plan is that he won't be able to get near you if he tries to come back."

"I feel so much better knowing that. And having guards posted all the time." For the first time since he arrived, he watched her truly relax.

"I'm afraid he's gotten himself into deep trouble. Trouble that none of us can take care of."

She tsked. "Quinton was such a sweet little boy. I don't know what happened. Maybe he made friends with the bad boys. By the time he was thirteen, his parents had a hard time with him. It almost broke my heart when his father had to send him away, but I understood. He was dangerous around the girls. We all thought he would straighten up and come home."

"I know I've laid an extra burden on you by asking you to shoulder even more responsibility."

She shook her head. "It's never a burden to care for those girls. I just wish I knew where our sweet Theresa was. If she's all right."

Wilson could at least take that burden from her. "I know where Theresa is, and I'm keeping her safe."

A soft smile crept over her face, and she sighed.

"I won't tell you where. Both to keep you safe and to keep her safe."

She nodded. "I understand, and what you told me relieves my heart."

A sudden idea entered his head. "Could you pack a suitcase with more of her things? I'll take it to her. She only had that one carpetbag."

For the first time, happiness shone from her eyes like a lighthouse on the shore. "Of course I will."

"Please be sure the other girls don't see you."

She nodded and hurried from the room.

When he left the Hilliard mansion, a suitcase for Traesa in hand, his heart was troubled. He wouldn't tell Traesa anything about the things he suspected until he knew for sure. If he was wrong and she'd never been adopted, he would have to help Traesa find a job and a place to stay. Old Mrs. Hilliard had adored the young woman, and he wouldn't be a very good lawyer if he didn't do all he could for her.

There *was* one other way he could help her, and it would benefit him at the same time, but was it feasible? Some clients thought he should be married to become more stable. And with all the things on the horizon for him and for her…marriage could be the answer for both of them.

He'd known of many couples who married for reasons other than love, and the marriages blossomed into beautiful lives together. That might happen with him and Traesa. She was a very pretty woman, and he'd seen her heart as she eased her grandmother's last years.

Love could come…eventually.

If he didn't come up with another alternative, he might have to suggest it. But what would the lovely Traesa think?

CHAPTER 5

*W*ilson had never imagined he'd be involved in such a troubling situation. By keeping Traesa's whereabouts from Mrs. Richards and her sisters, he caused them to worry about her. But he couldn't put her in more danger. A man as disturbed as Quinton might do anything imaginable...or unimaginable. Wilson had hired a security company, one known for skills and confidentiality, to protect those in the Hilliard mansion. The owner was a former Pinkerton agent, and he ran it with the integrity that Pinkerton did.

Wilson scheduled another guard to keep an eye on the boardinghouse during the day while he was at work. But he'd have to be the one to keep Traesa safe the rest of the time.

He felt like the juggler on stilts he'd seen at the Ringling Brothers Circus. Only he didn't know if he'd be able to keep everything up in the air and safe. *Lord, help me.*

Sometimes, he thought better on his feet, so he stood and paced the small space in his office. After lining up everything in his mind that he knew to be truth, a clearer picture emerged. He stopped behind the desk.

Glancing down at the will he found for Mrs. Hilliard and the document Quinton created, he saw so many discrepancies. Of course, he knew the wrinkled paper was a fake. The numbers included for Quinton and his two sisters were total fantasies. But the numbers on Mrs. Hilliard's will weren't much more accurate. She named everyone in the household with a bequest beside the name, but the estate was much larger than all the bequests combined. And Quinton was not even mentioned. He glanced at the date the will was signed—1890.

John and Mary Hilliard, her son and daughter-in-law, had died in 1891. They'd gone on a buggy ride out to their ranch on a warm spring day. Mr. Hilliard had been proud of his high-strung horses. They'd won races and awards. A farmer who raised pigs lived between their ranch and Fort Worth. One of his prize sows had escaped and lay asleep in the ditch beside the road. The clip-clop of the horses' hooves on the gravel road awoke the pig, and it snorted, causing the horse to run away.

John tried to stop him, but he couldn't. The buggy broke free from the horse, and John didn't let go of the reins until he'd been dragged far enough on the rocky soil that he couldn't hang on any longer. He was badly beaten up. The farmer saw the whole thing and ran for his wagon to check out John's injuries. In the meantime, the buggy careened down a hill and hit a picket fence. Mary was thrown and landed on two of the pointed boards. She died instantly. John died after they got him to the hospital. The accident seemed to have been all anybody talked about for weeks.

Wilson's mentor had told him the story when he introduced him to the Hilliard accounts. Wilson had understood at the time that the grandmother inherited everything, because her son and daughter-in-law knew she would take care of the children if anything happened to them at the same time. Since the grand-mother's assets would have been considerably higher after their deaths, she must have had a new will written. That would explain the discrepancy in her numbers. That was the main reason the will he had in his possession couldn't be the last will. He had to find a later one before he could read it to the heirs. This made his life even more complicated.

He went into the back room, where all the files were stored in wooden crates stacked six feet high. Narrow paths meandered among the stacks, and there was no rhyme or reason for where the information was located. It could take forever to find what he needed. While he searched, he could try to arrange the crates in such a way that he could find what he needed at a later time.

As he searched for the will, he'd keep an eye out for the adoption papers. He would also need to make sure the estate was maintained. The Hilliards had enough money and property to keep the household running for a long time.

❧

*T*raesa thanked Mr. Pollard for helping her, but she worried about him going to the mansion. What if Quinton tried to hurt him? Maybe even kill him. She gasped, and her heart clenched at the thought. Surely not. *Please God, don't let Quinton kill Mr. Pollard!*

She went to the window and glanced out. Since her room was at the back of the house, she couldn't see the street. Bright sunlight glistened on the melting ice that covered the ground, the trees, and roofs of houses. Of course, these extreme cold spells didn't last long here in Texas, and the water dripping from an icicle above showed it was already warming up outside.

She turned back toward the charming room. It felt a little like Abuela's room, with its beautiful quilt covering the bed, warm rugs, and cushioned rocking chair near the window. She pulled one of the books out of her carpetbag.

Little Lord Fauntleroy was the last book her grandmother had bought her. Traesa had only read the first chapter before Abuela's death. Since then, she hadn't taken time to read. She settled into the rocking chair and opened the book. Before long, she forgot about where she was, lost in the story.

When she finally looked up from the pages, the sun had moved at least two hours across the sky. Maybe she shouldn't have taken that much time away from the real world, but Abuela would have understood. There wasn't much she could do until Mr. Pollard returned. Except worry about her younger sisters and wonder if Quinton had done any more damage.

After laying the book on the table beside her chair, she paced. Along the way, she whispered a prayer. It was the only way she could help right now. But with every step she took, her burden felt heavier, not lighter. They needed help from God, but right now He felt a thousand miles away.

Tears streamed down her cheeks, so many she couldn't catch them all. Finally, she fell across the bed with her head buried in the soft pillow and sobbed. Every few minutes, she wiped her face with the hanky she'd tucked up her sleeve that morning. So long ago.

Soon sleep overtook her. When a knock on her door awakened her, the room was darker than when she'd fallen asleep.

"Coming." She hoped whoever was out there would wait while she splashed cool water from the pitcher over her warm cheeks.

When she glanced in the oval mirror on the wall above the pitcher and bowl, her eyes widened. She looked terrible, and there was no way to hide her reddened, swollen eyes. Clumps of hair had pulled loose, leaving curls clinging to her damp cheeks and neck.

"Miss Kildare?" Bridgett's voice sounded through the door.

After taking a deep breath, Traesa opened it.

Bridgett's gaze traveled over her face and form. "Oh, dear.

Do you need help preparing to go to supper? Mr. Pollard has chosen a table for the two of you."

Traesa nodded. "Can you really help me?"

"I think so." The other woman bustled into the room and closed the door. "Do you have another dress you can wear?"

"Yes." She hurried toward a stiff side chair that contained the layers of clothing she'd removed.

Bridgett followed and picked out a skirt and shirtwaist that matched and weren't too wrinkled. "Put these on, and I'll fix your hair. It won't take long." Her smile went straight to Traesa's heart. "Do you have any powder? If not, I have some in my room. It can cover some of the red around your eyes and on your cheeks."

"I didn't think I'd need the powder."

"I'll get mine while you change from your wrinkled clothes." She quickly slipped out the door.

While Bridgett fixed her hair and powdered her face, she kept up a stream of conversation that took Traesa's mind off her troubles. By the time they were finished preparing her to go downstairs, she felt more in control of her emotions.

As Traesa walked downstairs, she saw Wilson leaning against the wall just inside the boardinghouse, his legs crossed at the ankles and his hands stuck in the front pockets. He'd removed his jacket, and she noticed how his muscles filled out his shirt.

The thought made her blush. Why would she notice that? Never had a thought like that ever entered her mind...about any man.

~

*E*ven though her footsteps made no noise because of the carpeted steps, Wilson raised his head when Traesa came into view. Somehow he'd sensed her presence. Although he'd seen her numerous times when he'd visited Mrs. Hilliard, he'd never noticed what a beautiful woman she really was. When he'd first become the family lawyer, her hair had often been in corkscrew curls that flew around her head only restrained by a headband. Just a girl.

This evening, her regal carriage topped by a sophisticated hairdo startled him. For the first time, he understood what the Bible said when it referred to scales falling from eyes. Something shifted in his mind. That morning, he'd wanted to help her because of her grandmother. Now, he felt compelled to make sure nothing happened to her because of who *she* was. The woman he'd seen just as Mrs. Hilliard's granddaughter was so much more.

He pushed himself away from the wall and offered her his elbow. She slipped her soft hand through the opening, and he almost covered it with his other hand, but that wouldn't look right. People might get the wrong idea about their relationship, which was completely innocent…only business.

Molly led them toward a secluded table at the far end of the dining room. Hopefully, he could finish sharing what happened at the mansion before anyone needed to sit close to them.

Wilson pulled out her chair. After they were both seated, he glanced up at their waitress. "What's available tonight, Molly?"

"The special is meatloaf with scalloped potatoes, coleslaw, and hot rolls." She held her pencil above her writing pad.

Traesa smiled up at her. "That sounds delicious."

"Yes, it does. Bring us two orders."

"And tonight," Molly added, "we have molasses pie for dessert."

Just thinking about it made his mouth water. It was a favorite of his.

He sent a questioning glance toward Traesa, and she nodded. "And we'll have some to top off our meal."

Molly jotted the order on her pad. "Will you have whipped cream on your pie?"

"With."

"Without."

Both answers came at the same time.

"Okay, with for Mr. Pollard and without for Miss Kildare. I'll turn this order in and bring coffee or hot tea for you." She glanced at Traesa.

"I'll have the tea."

"And I'll have the coffee." He was ready for that since he'd been out in the cold so much today.

Molly brought their drinks out almost immediately.

Wilson put his hands around his mug to warm his fingers while Traesa took a sip of her tea.

"Abuela loved Earl Gray tea. It reminds me of her." She stared at him a moment before taking another sip.

For that momeToo soon worry wrinkles appeared between her eyebrows. So much had happened to her today, and he wasn't sure how soon he would be able to give her any good news.

nt, her eyes looked clear, and she wasn't frowning.

CHAPTER 6

*T*raesa walked into her room carrying the suitcase Mr. Pollard had brought earlier in the evening. She locked her door and set the case on the bed. His thoughtfulness surprised her, but it shouldn't have. After what she went through with Quinton, Mr. Pollard's kindness was a salve to her aching heart. The evening with the lawyer had been both interesting and disturbing. When he finished telling her what had transpired at the mansion, she didn't understand why it had happened.

Quinton should have been sober by the time Mr. Pollard showed up, but by the way he acted, he wasn't. The gall of the man, claiming to be the heir and making Mrs. Richards get some of the estate money for him. Whatever was he thinking? Of course, he was way beyond being able to think straight. Traesa had no idea what was going on in his life, and she didn't want to know, considering whatever he'd done had turned him into a monster. At least at that point, he was no longer in the house with her sisters. Even if they weren't blood kin, she couldn't stop loving them like the sisters they'd been for over eight years.

Knowing Mr. Pollard had appointed Mrs. Richards as their custodian helped calm some of Traesa's worries about them. She'd worried what would happen if Quinton returned until Mr. Pollard assured her that he had employed guards to protect both her and those at the mansion. She realized just how careful and caring the man was. Abuela would be pleased. She had liked him since the first time Mr. Harrison brought him out to meet her.

Traesa remembered that day clearly. From the very first time she'd seen Mr. Pollard, he'd impressed her, especially by the way he treated her grandmother. So respectful. So kind. So caring. Mr. Pollard was a good man. Mr. Harrison chose the right time to turn over the Hilliard account to him. It gave Mr. Pollard a year to get to know her grandmother and learn all about her business dealings before he passed away. Traesa didn't understand the business, because Abuelo had always met privately with him. She knew about the ranch, but that was all.

No one expected Mr. Harrison to die so soon after assigning the case to Mr. Pollard. She wondered if the older lawyer had already been ill when he did. Some people lived several years after finding out they were sick. Maybe he was making sure Mr. Pollard would have ample time to learn the Hilliard's businesses before he himself would be gone.

Traesa opened the brown leather case to find it filled with items she loved—three of her nicest dresses, which she hadn't packed because she thought she wouldn't need them as a working girl. There was other clothing, four more books, and some of the lovely figurines her grandmother had given her. She dropped beside the bed on her knees and held two of the figurines against her heart as tears streamed down her cheeks. Oh, how she missed Abuela. *God, why did she have to die?*

When she finished crying, she started to empty the bag. After setting the figurines on the table with the lamp, she hung the dresses on hooks in the armoire and folded her unmentionables and placed them in the drawers, along with more sleep-wear. She hadn't dug deep enough when she first opened the suitcase, because in the very bottom, she found a satin draw-string bag with many more pieces of jewelry Abuela had given her. Choosing to leave them had been a hard decision. Quinton probably had no idea all that her grandmother had given her, but she hadn't wanted to take a chance of him finding out she'd taken them and somehow punishing the younger girls for not keeping her from taking the valuables. Besides, when would she wear them if she was just a working girl?

Mrs. Richards had included a package of wrapped cookies. Snickerdoodles. The cookies she and Alice had been baking while Clara helped Traesa pack her carpetbag. She'd smelled the cinnamon when she exited the house.

While she soaked in the copper, claw-footed bathtub in the bathing room, all Traesa could think about were her sisters and the faithful housekeeper. Would she ever get to see them again, these people who were so precious to her?

~

*T*he night before, Wilson had returned to his office to search more of the crates. Mr. Harrison had been so good to him. He just wished the man had been more careful about the files. He hadn't gotten home until very late and then overslept and missed breakfast. He'd had the driver take him by a bakery on the way to the office. Hoping Traesa would be all right until the midday meal, he started on the other projects waiting on his desk while he consumed an enormous cinnamon roll along with a large cup of coffee. At least today the weather had settled back into spring instead of the winter feel of the day before.

After he finished the smaller projects, he started on a complex contract for a different client. The details were important. He'd sat hunched over the desk for two hours, and he was only half-way through. His back ached. As usual when he was stiff, he stood and stretched, then twisted side to side with his hands on his waist. He did ten twists, then stopped and walked around the office.

Just as he started a second set of ten twists, the front door opened.

"Pollard, are you finished with my contract?" His least favorite client, Mr. Westmoreland, frowned at him.

Wilson stepped back behind the desk. "I'm working on it right now. I'll be finished before the day is over."

"When I said I wanted it today, I thought you'd have it finished before now." The words sounded like a dog's growl.

Wilson bit back a snappy retort. "I fully intended to finish it yesterday, but I had to take care of an unexpected crisis with another client."

The older man stared around the office as if he'd never been there before. Wilson wondered what was bothering him now. The scowl never left the man's face. He couldn't remember him ever being so sour when Mr. Harrison was still alive. Something had his hackles up, and Wilson was sure he wouldn't like whatever he had to say.

After a loud harrumph, Westmoreland finally spoke. "I think your priorities are out of whack, Pollard. Harrison knew which side his bread was buttered on."

Wilson had been fulfilling all the man's demands since he'd been in charge of the law practice. Westmoreland had nothing to gripe about because the day wasn't over yet. He'd get his contract to him well before quitting time.

Westmoreland stared at Wilson. "Well, I reckon it mustn't have been too much of a crisis."

"How can you say that?" He tried to keep his temper in control. The man had no idea what he was talking about.

"That's the problem with young bachelors." The client gave a sharp nod. "I was meeting with an old friend at lunch yesterday. He lives in that boardinghouse. We saw you with a good-looking filly with red hair. Looked more like monkey business than a crisis to me. After this contract, I'm taking my legal business elsewhere. Never did think you was mature enough or settled enough to be a good lawyer."

Wilson stood speechless as the man rushed out the door and slammed it behind him. The nerve. Suggesting that he was dallying with Treasa's affections. Nothing could be farther from the truth. Not only was the man besmirching his good name, but he could damage Traesa's reputation too.

Just as I thought. More than one of his clients thought he should marry and settle down. He didn't want this law practice to fail. And he couldn't let Traesa's reputation be destroyed.

A glance at the clock showed he'd missed the noon meal at the boardinghouse, and he didn't know how Treasa was doing today. He'd have to wait to check on her. It would take till almost quitting time to finish this contract and deliver it to Westmoreland. His life just became more complicated. *Lord, I really need to know what You want me to do about Traesa...and the law practice.*

He was nearing the completion of the contract when his front door opened again. Jed Smith, the owner of the security firm, strolled in. The man gave a quick glance around the room. "You have quite a nice office here, Pollard."

Wilson stood. "How can I help you today?"

Jed dropped into one of the chairs across the desk from him, so he sat back down.

"I'm here to report on the matter you wanted me to personally look into." He leaned back and crossed one ankle over the other knee.

"And what did you find out? Anything helpful?"

Smith shook his head. "Not yet. But I'm sure there's something bad going on there. I've had some people tell me they know Quinton, but when I ask questions, they close up tight as a clam. No one has seen him for days, and a few of them seemed eager to find out if I know where he is. These aren't the kind of men I'd want to meet in an alley on a dark night, if you know what I mean."

Wilson huffed out a deep breath. "I sure do. I'm afraid he's in a lot of danger."

"I agree." Smith shook his head. "I don't often go into Hell's Half Acre. Most things going on down there are against the law, and even lawmen shy away from that place. Talk about the scum of the earth. Most everyone there fits into that category. It's a crying shame in a beautiful city like Fort Worth."

Wilson had wondered if Quinton would gather up the people he'd fired, as Wilson had demanded. He hadn't heard from the guards that he or anyone else had arrived at the mansion, and now he wasn't appearing where he'd been spending much of his time. Where could the young man be? Was he still alive?

"I know he's gotten himself in a lot of trouble," Wilson said. "Had you heard anything before about him?"

The man tapped his fingertips on the arms of the chair. "No. Just from you. I only opened my business here about two years ago. But I can tell you Quinton's in a whole lot of trouble. Sometimes, I went in places and asked questions. Other times, I kind of faded into the background and listened to what others were saying. I heard a couple of times that one of the business owners has his enforcer looking for Quinton. You know what that means."

Chills ran up and down Wilson's back. "I'm not familiar with the term 'enforcer.'"

"Well." Smith stroked his beard with one hand. "They're usually big, burly guys. Intimidating. And they use any method they need to get what their boss wants. I've heard of some breaking fingers or cutting them off. Even going so far as to cut off a hand...or some other body part. Sometimes, they leave dead bodies in alleys, and those are the lucky ones. Terrible business." He shook his head. "That's the part I don't cotton to in this business, having to deal with those kind of people. I wish all my clients only needed guards like you do."

Wilson knew Smith wasn't lying, but he couldn't fathom a man doing something like what the man described, even if he was being paid. A real man rescued and protected others.

He hoped he'd never have to find someone in Hell's Half Acre. "Why don't the Fort Worth city officials clean that place out? No city needs people like that...or places like those."

Smith shook his head. "I don't know. But there were places like Hell's Half Acre in many of the larger cities when I was with Pinkerton National Detective Agency. I think, if all those businesses are in the same area, decent folks can ignore what's going on. I saw things like that in plenty of other places, and they all contained the dregs of society. I try to push the bad things from my mind."

"I'm glad you opened your business here, and you're helping me keep the rest of the family safe. I just can't get Quinton out of my mind."

"From what I've heard, he's unforgettable."

"He was a real mess last time I saw him. What he did to his own family was unconscionable. I've held bad feelings against him. Wanted to take my fists to him for what he did to his adopted sister." He relaxed the fist he hadn't realized his right hand had made.

Wilson hoped it wouldn't be too late when they found him. His younger sisters would be devastated.

When he stood, so did Jed Smith. They shook hands.

"Glad to do business with you."

"Please let me know if you hear anything else about Quinton."

"Will do." The man headed out the door.

Wilson sat to finish the contract. He only had a paragraph to go. Then he could drop it off on the way to the boardinghouse. He just hoped Traesa had been all right today. After what she went through yesterday, he hadn't planned to leave her alone so long.

He didn't want to add to her worries. He had to come up with some way to really help her...and soon.

CHAPTER 7

*T*raesa knew Mr. Pollard was a busy man. He had other clients, and he'd spent so much time with her the day before. She'd looked forward to seeing him at breakfast, but he hadn't come before the dining room closed. She went upstairs and paced her room, wondering what was going on at the mansion. Were her sisters all right? Had Quinton returned? *Surely not.* She feared for their safety if he did.

Finally, she picked up *The Prince and the Pauper,* another book her grandmother bought for her. It sounded fascinating. Reading was better than worrying or pacing the floor. At least, she should see Mr. Pollard at the noon meal. Looking forward to that meeting, she sat in the chair beside the window and soon was lost in the story, so much that she almost forgot to go to dinner. A knock brought her out of the story.

When she opened the door, Bridgett stood in the hallway. "If you don't come down soon, you'll miss having some really good food."

Her smile warmed Traesa's heart, and her words brought a very unladylike growl from her stomach. Embarrassed, she tried to hide it with her hand, but it didn't work.

A wide smile crept across Bridgett's face. "It's a good thing I came, isn't it?"

She nodded and stepped out of her room. "Thank you for thinking of me. I got lost in a book." She pulled the door shut behind her.

As they hurried down the stairs, Bridgett turned toward her. "What book are you reading?"

"*The Prince and the Pauper* by Mark Twain. Do you like to read?"

Bridgett nodded. "I like to, but I don't have much time to."

"Have you read anything by Mark Twain?"

Bridgett stopped when they reached the bottom of the stairs. "Only *The Adventures of Tom Sawyer*. We read it in school."

They headed toward the dining room.

"He's written a lot of interesting books, and he's one of my favorite authors. My grandmother often bought me his stories." For a moment, her heart ached. If only she could see Abuela one more time. Tears formed in her eyes, but she blinked them back.

When they arrived at the entrance to the dining room, Traesa glanced around. She didn't see Mr. Pollard anywhere. She'd missed him again. Disappointment cloaked her like a heavy quilt.

"Bridgett, did Mr. Pollard already eat and leave?" she asked as they walked into the dining room, where only a few people still sat at tables.

Bridgett shook her head, worry puckering her forehead. "Actually, I haven't seen him at all today. It's unusual for him to miss a meal, much less two in a row."

As Molly approached the young women, a smile spread across her face. "Where would you like to sit, Miss Kildare?"

Traesa's gaze swept over the room. "I'm not sure."

"I haven't eaten yet." Bridgett took a step closer to Traesa. "Why don't we share the meal? That way you won't have to eat alone, and I'd love to get to know you better."

Traesa nodded, and Molly led them to a table by the front windows. "How about here?"

They took their places across from each other in the chairs closest to the window. Bright sunlight warmed the area. It bathed the neighborhood in a golden glow, hopefully signaling the end of the unseasonable cold spell. Since she'd lived in Texas for over eight years, Traesa knew the weather was a bit crazy sometimes. But in all those years, it had never been as cold this late in spring as yesterday had been.

"It's good to see you, Miss Kildare." Molly took her notepad and pencil from her apron pocket. "I'm afraid you missed out on the smothered pork chops. They're all gone, but we still have chicken pot pie. Would you like rolls or cornbread with it?"

With so much flaky crust on the top, Traesa decided not to have either.

Molly scribbled on the paper. "What about fried apples with that?"

Traesa was hungry, and she really liked the dish rich with cinnamon and butter. "Yes, please." Her mouth began to water.

"What would you like to drink?" Molly's pencil still poised over the pad.

"Milk, if you have some."

"Sure do." Molly wrote that down and turned toward Bridgett.

"What she's having sounds good to me."

"Thank you." Molly gave them another wide smile. "I'll have this right out for the two of you."

Traesa watched the cheerful woman head to the kitchen then turned toward her companion. "I'll be through with the book soon. You can borrow it if you'd like."

"Thank you. Maybe I can read it in the evenings when I get off work." She took the napkin from under her silverware and spread it across her lap.

Traesa followed suit.

Bridgett clasped her hands on the table. "Could I ask you a question?"

Hoping it wouldn't be too personal, she said, "Yes."

"I noticed you with Mr. Pollard. And now you've asked about him. Is he…a special…friend? If you know what I mean."

From Bridgett's sweet smile, Traesa knew she didn't mean anything bad, but she did ask a very personal question. How should she answer?

She took a deep breath. "He was my grandmother's lawyer. She passed away recently, and he's now our family lawyer. He's helping me out."

That should take care of the question without giving away too much information.

"Oh."

Before Bridgett could say anything else, Molly returned and set a glass of milk in front of each of them.

Bridgett watched her go before turning back toward Traesa. "He was so concerned about you. I thought maybe you were interested in each other."

For a moment, all Traesa could think about was how handsome Mr. Pollard was. He was tall and with all that dark wavy hair and those hazel eyes, she did feel drawn to him. She hadn't thought of him the way Bridgett was talking about before, but in other circumstances, she could be interested in a different kind of relationship with him. She felt as if a whole flock of butterflies took flight in her stomach.

Thank goodness, Molly returned with their plates, saving her from responding to Bridgett's comment.

"Thank you, Molly. This smells so good. I'm glad I didn't miss dinner." After taking her first bite of the delicious chicken and vegetables, she decided to change the subject. "How long have you worked here at the boardinghouse?"

When Bridgett answered, she knew she had dodged that last

comment. Now all she had to do was keep asking her questions, not giving her the chance to ask any more.

~

*I*f Wilson was going to get any supper, he had to hurry. After the day he'd had, he was starved. And he wanted to see how Traesa was faring. He didn't even take time to freshen up before heading to the dining room. His eyes were immediately drawn toward Traesa sitting near the fireplace. With a pensive far-away expression, she stared out the window at the fading twilight. He wondered what she was thinking about.

He started across the room, but Molly reached her first. They greeted each other with a smile while the waitress refilled her drink. He hoped she was as eager to see him as he was to see her. He wished he had better news for her.

Several of the men who lived in the boarding house stopped him with a greeting as he made his way among the tables. By the time he reached her, she had just taken her first bite.

"Traesa."

Her gaze quickly turned to him, and joy filled her eyes.

"May I join you?"

"Of course." Warmth infused her tone.

He pulled out a chair on the side nearest Traesa. "How have you been today?"

Her smile faltered for an instant. If he hadn't been looking right at her, he wouldn't have seen it. Maybe her day hadn't been so good. All he could do was apologize for not seeing her sooner. Perhaps that would be enough.

Molly arrived with her pad and pencil. "Wilson, we missed you earlier."

"And I missed being here. I worked late yesterday and accidentally slept late this morning. I had to get something from the bakery for breakfast, and I missed dinner completely."

"This meatloaf is so good," Traesa said, "even better than the wonderful meatloaf Mrs. Benton makes."

He nodded to Molly. "Please, bring me what she's having."

"Okay." She whirled around and left.

He huffed out a big breath. "I'm sorry I wasn't here before."

She looked down at her food. "That's all right."

By her tone, he knew it wasn't. "I was up really late last night, because I was trying to find the right files to prove your adoption. And I don't think I have the last will from your grandmother. Things don't make sense."

He stopped talking. He was just making excuses, and that's not what he wanted to do. He wanted to focus on Traesa and what she needed right now. "What did you do today?"

She pushed the food around on her plate as if she were inspecting it. She didn't take a bite. "I read quite a bit and took a nap." She laid her fork carefully on the edge of her plate. "I did miss seeing you at breakfast and dinner. I'm glad you're here for supper."

What exactly did she mean by that? He wished he knew. There seemed to be a deeper meaning to her words. But what? A headache started at the base of his skull and moved upward. Was it just because he'd missed a meal, or was it because of all the pressure he was feeling?

He rubbed the back of his neck with one hand. "I had to write a special contract for another of my clients. He didn't like the fact that I hadn't finished it this morning."

Molly brought his food, and he thanked her. He only took one bite before continuing.

"The owner of the security company came by to make a report on Quinton." He noticed her shiver when he mentioned her brother, so he hurried on. "He's been searching for him. Even went to Hell's Half Acre because we thought Quinton might be in trouble down there. People knew him, but no one had seen him lately. Finding him might be a lost cause."

She heaved a sigh that sounded like relief. Perhaps she didn't want to find him, and maybe she was right. How could Quinton do anything to help with the situation they found themselves in? At this point, Wilson wanted rape charges brought against the man.

"Mr. Pollard, I can't just stay here and do nothing." Before he could swallow, she continued. "I need something positive to keep me busy. Can you arrange that?"

He wanted to say he could, but he had no idea what. "Will you be all right here for a couple more days at least?"

She took another bite and got a faraway look in her eyes. Perhaps she was mulling over his question. What would he do if she didn't agree? His hands began to sweat. While she was staring out the window, he wiped them on his trousers. *Lord, I need some help down here.*

He really had his hands full. Tomorrow he needed to go out to the mansion to check in with Mrs. Richards.

~

*T*raesa paced her room, trying to make sense of all that had happened. Mr. Pollard had no idea when he'd be able to read the will, so she didn't know whether she was mentioned in it.

What if she wasn't? As soon as the will was read, she'd no longer be supported by the estate money. What could she do then?

She pulled all the money she owned from the drawer where she'd hid it. Such a paltry sum. Not nearly enough for her to live on. Or even to get a place to live. If she went into service in one of the other cattle baron mansions, what would she do? Not many of them had children young enough to need a nanny or even a tutor.

She got the jewelry she'd brought and what Mrs. Richards had sent and splayed the pieces across the bed beside her too small funds. All of them together wouldn't take her through many days or weeks.

Her future looked hopeless. Tears overflowed her eyes and flooded down her cheeks.

CHAPTER 8

*W*ilson noticed Mary Kelley watching him hurry between the tables toward the lobby of her boardinghouse. "Good Morning, Mary. I see Miss Kildare hasn't arrived for breakfast."

"I want to talk to you before you see her. Shall we go into the parlor?" She gestured toward the room on the other side of the lobby.

"Sure." He followed her.

After she sat in the middle of the sofa with green brocade upholstery, he dropped into the matching wingback chair. He hoped nothing had happened to Traesa. She didn't need to go through any major trauma so soon after the attempted rape.

"What can I do for you?" He leaned his forearms on his thighs and watched Mary's expression. She didn't look too concerned. Maybe he didn't have anything to worry about.

"I really don't want to be bearing tales, but I thought you should know what's been going on. This will be just between the two of us. Right?" She loosely clasped her hands in her lap.

"Of course."

"The last two nights, Traesa has had bad nightmares." She shifted her feet on the carpet.

"How do you know? Did she tell you?" He couldn't imagine that.

She shook her head. "No. My room is right under hers. I heard her. She cried out in her sleep then sobbed into her pillow. I was afraid something terrible was wrong with her, so I went into her room. She hadn't awakened, but when I sat on the side of her bed, she did."

"I see." But actually, he didn't. He hoped it wasn't about her attack, but it probably was.

"I took her in my arms, and she grabbed my robe in her fists and held on for dear life and sobbed. I tried to calm her by rubbing her back as I did with my daughter when she had a nightmare. Before long, she settled down and went back to sleep. I'm not sure she even remembers it. She didn't say anything about it yesterday."

The words gripped his heart. He never wanted Traesa to be hurt in any way. All he wanted was to keep her safe. Evidently, Quinton's abuse affected her more than he'd realized. He couldn't destroy her confidence in him by revealing her secrets to Mrs. Kelley. His emotions and thoughts were in disarray, trying to make sense of it all and to come up with a permanent solution to the problem.

"There's another thing, Wilson. She's unhappy in the daytime, too. She tries to hide it, but I can tell." She leaned toward him. "I have no idea why you brought her here, and I don't want to know, but we need to help her...somehow."

"I agree." He rubbed his jaw with one hand. "She did tell me last night at supper that she wanted something to do. She's not used to being inactive. I brought her here for her protection. That's all I can tell you. She doesn't need to be seen out and about in town. I have no idea how to help her find something to occupy her mind."

The sounds of people entering the dining room drifted into the parlor.

Mary stood. "I have to go help with serving breakfast now. Maybe we can talk about this again."

His gaze followed her as she left the room. Why did the owner have to help serve the meals? An idea started to form in his mind. Maybe there was a way to help Traesa without her even knowing why.

~

*W*hen Traesa came down the stairs, her gaze was drawn to Mr. Pollard leaning on the wall beside the door with his ankles crossed. Just the way she'd seen him that first day he brought her to the boardinghouse. A smile crept over her face. Was he waiting for her? She hoped so.

He stood up straight with one arm crooked toward her. "Miss Kildare, may I escort you to breakfast?"

"Of course." She slid her hand through the elbow and along his muscular forearm. The pleasing scent of Bay Rum Oil, which Mr. Hilliard had used when he shaved, wafted around Mr. Pollard. She could tell he'd combed his hair, but one wave almost touched his forehead. She wanted to push it back from his face. *Wonder what he'd do if I did.*

"Where would you like to sit?"

She glanced around the rapidly filling room. "There's an empty table beside the windows. I like to look at the sunshine, and what shines through the window helps warm me up."

Mr. Pollard placed his hand gently against her back as he escorted her to the table. The heat from that started warmth moving through her body. He pulled out the chair on one side of the table for her before taking his place facing her.

~

"*H*ow are you doing today?" *Will she tell me about her nightmares?*

"Fine."

He could help her more if she would share what she felt, but with everything that had happened, he understood why she might not.

"I love mornings. Everything is bright, and we have a chance for a new start."

That was one way to look at it. But did she really believe that? He had no way of knowing unless she told him more.

"Just this morning as I was reading my Bible and praying, I found a verse that said God's mercies are new every morning, because He is faithful. I will keep those words in my thoughts today." She smiled as Molly approached.

He turned his attention to the waitress. "What's for breakfast?"

"Besides the usual eggs, today we have bacon and biscuits. And we have a special treat. Buckwheat cakes and molasses. I've always loved them."

"I couldn't possibly eat as much as he is, but I want to try the buckwheat pancakes. That will be all for me. Oh, and I want milk with mine."

"And I'll have coffee."

Molly left to get their drinks.

When she was far enough away to not hear their conversation, he leaned toward Traesa. "Yesterday, you told me you want something to do to keep busy. I really don't want you going out anywhere without me. Danger is still lurking outside. But I noticed Mrs. Kelley helping serve breakfast. She hasn't done that before." He gave a quick glance around the room. "More and more people who don't live in the boardinghouses are eating here. If you agree to it, we can ask her if she needs any help. That could give you something to do."

Traesa's eyes widened as if he had surprised her, and she didn't say anything right away. He hoped he hadn't offended her. Maybe that wasn't something she'd want to do. He'd never had to handle anything like this for a client. And he sure didn't understand how a woman's mind worked.

"That might be a good idea. Maybe I could help here in the dining room...or the kitchen...or even cleaning rooms. Something like that." A smile lit her eyes.

"Did you do those kinds of things for the Hilliard family?"

"No, but I know how. I was twelve years old when I came to Fort Worth on the orphan train. My mother taught me a lot about keeping a house and caring for a family before she and my father died. Often Abuela didn't want the maids doing her room when she wasn't feeling well. I was able to get it cleaned without bothering her."

"When we finish eating, I need to go check on things at the mansion. That won't take long. When I'm finished, I'll see if Mrs. Kelley has time for us to talk to her. We can ask her about you helping out then."

~

Wilson kept his horse Golden Girl in the stable behind the boardinghouse, as several of the other men did. The morning was even milder than yesterday's had been. A good day for a ride. As he saddled his mare, he often talked to her. Just as he started to, another man came in.

"Good day to ya." The man tipped his hat.

Wilson nodded back at him. "Good day for a ride."

The other man started to saddle his paint horse. "I sure was glad to find a boardinghouse with a stable. I don't really like taking those hansom cabs, and the livery stable is too far to walk to."

"I only use a cab in bad weather or when I'm escorting someone else."

The man held his saddle in place with both arms. "Like the lady with you at breakfast."

Wilson mounted his horse. "I'm a lawyer. She's a client."

He wheeled around and rode out the open stable door. He wasn't sure, but he thought the man had a smirk on his face. He hoped not. Traesa's reputation must be protected at all costs.

There was activity at the Hilliard mansion when he rode up. George Benton and Mr. Richards were working together to remove fallen leaves and other debris from the flower gardens and the front lawn. They stopped what they were doing and watched him as he approached the front porch.

Mr. Richards walked toward him when he dismounted. "A good day to you, Mr. Pollard. I'll take your horse."

"I won't be long, so I'll just tie her to the hitching post. I'm glad you and Mr. Benson are back at work."

"According to my wife, thanks to you. And I'm mighty thankful."

Wilson held out his hand. "I'm happy I could be a help." Mr. Richards had a strong grip. He liked that in a man.

He headed up the steps to the porch. Before he could ring the doorbell, the door opened. Smythe gave him a wide smile. "Welcome, Mr. Pollard."

"I'm glad to see you back at work too. I missed you when I came out here before."

The butler held the door open wide. "Thank you for getting our jobs back for us."

"You're welcome. Glad to help." He hung his hat on the hall tree. "Where will I find Mrs. Richards?"

"I believe she's in her office right now, sir."

As he walked toward the back of the first floor, he glanced into each open doorway.

The two maids were cleaning in different rooms. Everything

looked to be in order, with nothing missing. The two girls sat in the parlor working on some kind of needlework. They didn't even look up when he strode by. Before he reached the kitchen, he savored the aroma of whatever Mrs. Benton was cooking for their noon meal. She looked up and nodded a greeting to him.

He knocked on the door facing of the housekeeper's office. She looked up and waved him in.

"It's good to see everyone taking care of the place." He dropped into the chair across the desk from her.

"It's all because of you."

"Only doing my job." He leaned his elbows on the arms of the wingback chair. "How are things going?"

She smiled at him. "Almost back to normal."

"I take it you haven't heard from Quinton."

She nodded. "Have you found out anything?"

He caught Mrs. Richards up on what he learned. "Evidently, he's hiding somewhere else. We have no idea where."

She glanced down at her hands clasped on the top of her desk. "In a way, I'm glad. But in another way, I'm not. Without us knowing where he is, our Theresa can't come back to us. It's a real dilemma."

"That it is." He huffed out a deep breath. "I'm doing everything possible to find him. Until then, we have help protecting her and all of you."

He reached into the inside pocket of his suit coat and removed an envelope. "I've brought you more household money. I don't want you to run low. And remember, don't hesitate to let me know if you need anything. The estate has plenty of money in the bank." He laid it on her desk.

"Thank you." She took the envelope and locked it in one of the desk drawers without even looking in it. He was surprised. He'd expected her to count it before she did that.

"Now I have another matter to discuss."

She looked up, a question in her gaze.

LENA NELSON DOOLEY

"Since I have to keep Theresa hidden to protect her, could you pack more of her belongings for me to take to where she is staying? More clothing and more of her books. Things like that. I rode my horse, so I'll have to come back with a cab to take them to her."

"Is she doing all right?"

He could see how much she really loved Traesa. "So far."

"I'll pack everything I can get in two of the family suitcases. Mrs. Hilliard had several pieces of luggage for when they traveled."

Wilson whistled a tune as he went back outside. At least some things were looking up. He untied the reins from the hitching post and rode back toward the boardinghouse. *Where could Quinton be?* He didn't want him near Traesa or the others at the mansion, but he wanted to know where the man was.

Or if he was even still alive.

CHAPTER 9

*T*raesa straightened up her room then sat by the window to read until Mr. Pollard returned. Seeing him was always the brightest spot in her day.

After reading three chapters, she stood and gazed out the window, not really noticing the view. Her thoughts turned to the wonderful man who'd stepped in like a knight in shining armor to save her from the dismal future she faced. She still had no idea what would happen now, but she knew Wilson was trustworthy. If only they could find something productive for her to do while she waited.

A gentle knock sounded on her door. "Traesa, are you here?"

Bridgett's voice was soft. Maybe she thought Treasa was asleep.

"Yes." She hurried across the room and pulled open the door. "Come in."

Since she hadn't been able to go to church after Abuela became too sick to attend, her so-called friends there had faded away. Not really friends at all. *Is there something about me that keeps me from making true friends?* She hoped not. Right now, Bridgett was the closest thing she had to a friend.

"Mr. Pollard is waiting for you in the parlor." A smile spread across her friend's face as she stepped back so Traesa had room to get by. "He sounded eager to see you."

By the way Bridgett's eyes twinkled, Traesa knew what she was thinking. But she was very wrong in her assessment of the situation. Of course, Traesa wouldn't turn down a different kind of relationship between them, but he was her grandmother's lawyer not her beau.

"Thank you."

After pulling the door closed behind her, she accompanied Bridgett down the staircase to the foyer of the boardinghouse. Bridgett continued on to the dining room while Traesa entered the parlor.

A welcoming smile from Wilson brought one to her face too. "Mr. Pollard, so glad to see you. How did everything go?" She sat in the wingback chair across from him and clasped her hands in her lap.

"I had a good visit with Mrs. Richards." He crossed one knee over the other as he leaned back in the chair. "They haven't seen or heard from Quinton."

She frowned. "That's good, isn't it?"

"For now, yes. Clara and Alice are doing needlework today. I asked Mrs. Richards to pack more of your things so I could bring them to you. That's why I was gone so long. I had ridden Golden Girl, and had to bring her back and have a cab take me to bring the luggage." He gestured toward the two suitcases she hadn't noticed on the other side of his chair.

"Thank you." She wondered what all she would find in these pieces of luggage.

It would be nice to have more of her possessions. She'd feel more normal, not as if she were some kind of runaway who needed to hide from the world. *But I do need to hide from Quinton.* A shiver ran up her spine.

His foot thudded to the floor, and he leaned toward her. "I think I've worked out your other problem, too."

What other problem?

"I had a little visit with Mrs. Kelley before I sent for you. She liked the idea of you helping in the dining room and kitchen."

"She did?" Maybe it would keep her from worrying so much and keep her occupied until he returned each day.

"It will keep her from having to work in the dining room. After all, she has a boardinghouse to run. But she only agreed if you'll let her pay you as she would any employee."

Traesa hadn't had to worry about money since she was adop —since she'd come to live with the Hilliard family. Abuela made sure she had spending money. Traesa had saved most of what she gave her, because her grandmother paid for everything when they went out together. Traesa hadn't had anything else to spend her money on, which was why she'd had the funds she brought when she left the mansion. Being able to add to that total was a good idea. She had no idea what was in her future. She might need the extra money somewhere down the line.

"I'd like that." She gave him a smile, and he returned one, causing a hitch in her heartbeat.

"She said you can start today, if you'd like to."

Would she ever! "What time?"

"If you want to help with the noon meal crowd, you can start then. That will give you time to unpack your bags. She doesn't need you for another hour." He stood.

She did, too. "I'd like to see what Mrs. Richards sent this time."

"Would they let me carry the luggage up to your room?" He picked up both bags. "One of them is rather heavy."

She shrugged. "I don't know. You'll have to ask."

After he obtained Mrs. Kelley's permission, he accompanied Traesa to her room and set both suitcases on the bed. "I have a lot to do at the office."

After a quick wave, he was gone.

Traesa hurried to open the baggage. She felt as if it was her birthday or Christmas as she unloaded more clothes, books, knickknacks, and another package of snickerdoodles. That extra treat made her realize how much she was loved. Quinton couldn't take that away from her. Maybe Wilson would take her back to the house sometime so she could see the girls and Mrs. Richards.

~

*W*ilson's heart lifted seeing Traesa so happy. It eased his mind, and he was able to work without worrying so much about her. Even with all the time he'd spent going through the files in the back room, making sure the documents he opened were stored in alphabetical order after he perused them, he was no closer to finding what he needed to settle the Hilliard estate. After he'd spent another hour in the files, he heard the office door open.

Quickly, he went to see who arrived. He wasn't sure he recognized the man who stood looking around the office as if he'd never been there before.

"May I help you?" He used his most professional tone.

"You're the young lawyer Mr. Harrison hired, aren't you?" The man gave him a once-over without even a hint of a smile on his face.

"Yes, sir. Are you one of his clients? I don't think I've met you before." Wilson tried not to grit his teeth. This man wasn't the least bit friendly.

"He's done some work for me in the past. I heard about you from one of my friends. He suggested that I might want to pick up my files from you and take them to another lawyer he recommended in town."

This didn't bode well. That was two clients who were changing lawyers. If many more did, it could ruin the firm.

"Usually, we send the files to the new lawyer directly. If you'll give me the address, I'll make sure he has them first thing in the morning."

An ugly frown glared back at him. "If you're sure you can get them there by then, all right. Do you have a note pad?"

Wilson handed it and a pencil to the man, and he scribbled the address on the paper. Then he strode out the door with heavy footsteps, and he wasn't gentle closing the door either. Maybe it was a good thing he was taking his business elsewhere. Trying to work with him would quickly get tiresome.

He spent another hour going through files before someone entered the office again. When he stepped into the main room, he found Jed Smith.

"Do you have another report for me? I hope it's a good one." He shook hands with the owner of the security company. "Have a seat." He gestured to one of the chairs across from his desk. When the other man was seated, Wilson dropped into the second chair.

"I have a report, but I'm not sure whether you'll consider it good or not."

"Let's have it."

Jed sat with his elbows on the arms of the chair and his fingers tented in front of him. "None of the men guarding the boardinghouse and the mansion have seen Quinton."

"That sounds good to me." This was just what he wanted to hear, that everyone was safe.

"I've kept men searching for him, especially in Hell's Half Acre, but other places as well. We're not sure, but a vagrant has been walking by this office off and on for several days. He doesn't come to the door. He slinks around the building as if looking for something. My men aren't sure it's Quinton. He kind of looks like him, but he's looking really bad. Unkempt hair. A really rank smell accompanies him, and he's worn the same filthy clothes every day."

"When did this happen? Is he still coming around?"

Wilson didn't want Quinton near his office. If the scoundrel hid and followed when he went home, he would be leading him straight to Traesa. That would be a disaster.

Jed dropped his hands into his lap and leaned forward. "Today the same man was seen at the back door of the boardinghouse. We don't know if he's looking for Miss Kildare, or not."

"That is too close for comfort, to be sure. What do we do now?"

"We'll keep a close eye on him. We won't let him get inside. My man will do a citizen's arrest if he has to." Jed stood. "I'll let you know if anything else happens."

They shook hands, and he exited.

Wilson grabbed his coat and headed out the door for the boardinghouse.

He barely made it before they stopped serving the noon meal, and only a few people were still eating. After he sat at an empty table, Traesa came to serve him.

"The only thing left to eat is some beef stew and rolls. I hope that's all right with you." She smiled at him.

His stomach let him know just how empty it was. "I'll take whatever you have."

"I think we have some chocolate cake left too. That would be a tasty ending for your meal." She turned to leave.

"Miss Kildare."

She turned back with her eyebrows lifted. "Yes."

"Have you eaten?" He sure hoped not. He really wanted to talk to her. For more reasons than one.

"Mrs. Kelley said I can eat now. You are the last person I need to serve."

"Good. Bring your meal out and eat with me. I want to know how your first morning to help has gone."

Soon she returned carrying a loaded tray. After setting the food in front of him and the chair where she would sit, she put the tray on the opposite corner of the table.

Molly followed her with a tray containing their drinks and the cake. She took the other empty tray with her when she returned to the kitchen.

Wilson turned toward Traesa. "Do you mind if I say a blessing over our food?"

"Go right ahead." She bowed her head with her hands in her lap.

After he said, "Amen," she echoed it.

The food was delicious, as always. "How has your morning gone?"

"It felt wonderful to be doing something productive. So freeing. I've been feeling almost like a prisoner since I arrived here." She touched his arm. "I know that's not what you were doing, making me a prisoner. You were protecting me, and I appreciate it."

Her hand felt warm even through his clothing. When she lifted it, his arm felt almost cold. Strange.

"So what have you done so far?" He continued to eat while she answered.

"I spent some time in the kitchen with Mrs. Saunders. I helped prepare the vegetables she used in the stew and other things like that. It's reminding me of some of the things my mother taught me. I really didn't do much cooking when I was with the Hilliards." She took another bite.

He glanced toward the kitchen. "I'm sure you enjoyed it."

"Later she will be teaching me how to bake pies and cakes. I'm excited about that." The twinkle in her eyes confirmed the words she spoke.

"Did anything else interesting happen?"

"Not really." She had a thoughtful expression on her face. "There is one thing they do in the kitchen I like a lot."

He put his spoon on the side of his plate. "What's that?"

"I hadn't realized how many people there are who don't have jobs here in Fort Worth." She frowned. "Before I came west on the Orphan Train, I had to scavenge for food in New York City. It was horrible. There were quite a few children who did. We helped each other. Mrs. Kelley and Mrs. Crawford always have food available when anyone comes to the kitchen door asking for something to eat."

His heart almost stopped beating. Surely, Quinton hadn't seen Traesa in the kitchen. *Please, God, no. Protect her.*

"A man came while we were making the rolls." She took a bite of hers. "I didn't see him, but I heard the voices murmuring. I asked Mrs. Saunders what was going on, and she told me about the aid they provide for those in dire straits. I respect them for providing a service like that."

If the man who was seen going behind the boardinghouse had been Quinton, at least he hadn't seen Traesa. He had to figure a way to keep her safe from the wretch. They had no way of knowing when the man would return. He needed to make sure there was no way for him to see her when he did.

CHAPTER 10

MAY

*A*fter a quiet day when Traesa only saw Wilson at mealtimes, she awoke eager to get to work again. She glanced out the window and saw bright sunshine and leaf buds on the trees. At least May brought the kind of weather that was usual for spring in Texas.

Today, she would be doing a few more things on her own. She felt useful, and she wanted to learn much more.

As she started down the stairs, Bridgett joined her. "I'm so glad you're working here. How do you like it?"

"A lot." Traesa smiled at her. "Mrs. Sanders has taught me so much in the time I've been working with her. And she's so kind when I make a mistake."

Bridgett held the banister as they approached the foyer. "This has been the best place I've ever worked too."

At the bottom of the stairs, they parted. Bridgett to clean the rooms and change the linens and Traesa to work in the kitchen. The inviting aromas that wafted around the first floor aroused her hunger.

"Good morning, everyone."

She picked up a fresh apron that covered the ruffles on the front of her waist and fell almost to the floor over her skirt. She had needed that much coverage yesterday. Maybe today, she wouldn't get the apron as dirty as she had been.

Mrs. Sanders turned from the stove and smiled at her. "Good morning. Do you think you're ready to make the biscuits by yourself this morning?"

She took a deep breath and let it out slowly. "I am."

"Okay, everything is waiting for you on that cabinet." The cook gestured to the one on the other side of the stove with the larger oven.

Traesa hurried over and began sifting flour into a large bowl. If she'd been alone, she'd have started singing. Happiness bubbled inside her. She glanced at the recipe at every step to make sure she did everything in the right order. After she had the dough gently mixed, she turned it out on the floured board then sprinkled a little flour on the top. With the waiting rolling pin, she smoothed the large lump of dough until it was the correct thickness.

"How are you doing?" Mrs. Sanders called across the kitchen.

"Just fine."

Traesa glanced around, looking for the tin can they used to cut the biscuits into even sizes. Spying it on a shelf where the other dry ingredients were stored, she retrieved it and started to work, cutting the biscuits as close to each other as she could to keep from wasting dough.

A knock sounded at the back door, and a rough, masculine voice called, "Got any food for me today?"

Sheila, the cook's helper, gathered up some leftovers from yesterday and went to open the door.

Traesa saw the unkempt man who stood in the open doorway. *Poor man.* She remembered how hard it had been to get anything good to eat when she was an orphan in New York City. Often, she and some of the other children had had to dig through the garbage to get a scrap of food. There hadn't been even one place like this that gave food to the needy, and she and her friends had been very needy.

She placed the last biscuit on the baking pan and turned to put it in the oven. The man glanced toward her, and their gazes collided. She would recognize those eyes anywhere. *Quinton!* Her heartbeat accelerated, and she could hardly breathe.

Her first inclination was to turn and run, but instead she stared at him as if frozen. She clutched the edges of the pan tight to keep from losing the biscuits.

Recognition entered his eyes. "Theresa?"

With a flash of fear in his gaze, he grabbed the flour bag of food. Without another word, he whirled and ran.

Almost immediately, a man Traesa had never seen before ran the same direction. She didn't know where he came from. He certainly didn't look homeless. Why was he chasing Quinton? What was he going to do if he caught him? She shouldn't care, but she did.

She didn't want the man she'd grown up with to be killed, but she also didn't want to see him ever again. She was shaking like a leaf in a strong wind. Quickly, she shoved the pan into the hot oven and closed the door.

Mrs. Sanders came across the kitchen to her side. She placed an arm around Traesa and helped her sit. "Are you all right, Traesa?"

"I will be."

The beggar at the door looked far worse than the man who had attempted to rape her. She never wanted to see that man again, but she hadn't wished him dead. Evidently, Quinton didn't have money to get any liquor now. Although he left a malodorous smell lingering in the doorway, she didn't detect even a hint of alcohol in it.

Who was he hiding from? And who was the man chasing him? She wondered if Wilson would have any idea what was going on. Maybe she could talk to him at breakfast about what happened.

~

*W*ilson had grabbed a quick cup of coffee before he left for his office. He'd bought cheese and crackers to keep there so he didn't have to take the time to eat a full breakfast. He could take time for dinner with Traesa before he came back to the office for the afternoon.

A client had arrived at the office late the day before needing a contract written by noon today. Having a new client gave him hope. Maybe the two who'd left the firm were the only ones who didn't think he could be a good lawyer as a single young man. He certainly hoped so.

He had been writing the legal document for about an hour when a man burst through the front door, slamming it back against the wall. He leaned against the door facing, breathing deeply.

Wilson jumped up and hurried toward him.

It was the agent who was supposed to be guarding the boardinghouse.

"Why are you here?" He didn't intend to sound so sharp, but he had to know if everything was all right with Traesa.

The guard took a moment to catch his breath.

"Do you need to sit down?"

He shook his head then swallowed, his Adam's apple bobbing with the effort. "Jed told me to come tell you if anything happened."

"Well, out with it." Wilson held his breath as all kinds of terrible things raced through his mind. He forced out a breath to calm his elevated heartbeat.

"A bum who's been hiding out near the boardinghouse looks like he might be Quinton. His clothes are filthy, and he hasn't shaved or bathed since we first noticed him. He must be sleeping outside somewhere."

"What did he do?" Wilson wanted to shake the words out of the man, but he held his anger in check by clenching his fists and shoving them in the pockets of his slacks.

"I saw him at the back door. It all seemed normal until he sprinted away. I ran after him."

Good. Finally, Wilson would be able to talk to Quinton again. Find out what he was doing and what kind of trouble he was in.

"So where is he?"

This guard was taking entirely too long to get to the point.

"I don't know."

"You don't know?" Ire arose inside Wilson. He had a hard time trying to tamp it down. "How could you not know?"

"He ran along the Trinity River then turned into a forested area thick with underbrush. I tried to catch him, but by the time I reached the forest, he had disappeared. I searched and searched, but never found any trace of where he'd gone. So I hurried over here to tell you."

"Thank you. Please go back to your post at the boarding-house. I don't want Traesa unprotected."

A frown veiled the man's face. "What did you say?"

Wilson took a deep breath. "I said to go back—"

"What name did you use?"

"Traesa. She's the reason I hired you."

He hoped the guard would leave quickly. He still had quite a bit to write before noon.

"The bum said something like that before he ran. It sounded like Theresa to me."

It was Quinton, for sure.

After the guard left, Wilson called the investigator. As soon as Jed answered, he said, "We know where Quinton is." Wilson tapped his foot on the floor.

If only he could go looking for him, but he had to finish this contract. He couldn't afford to lose the new client.

Wilson explained what the guard had told him, and Jed agreed to send out a team to comb the woods.

When he hung up, he had a hard time concentrating, and he barely finished the contract before the client came to pick it up.

After looking it over, the client thanked him, paid him, and left with the envelope in his hand.

Finally, Wilson could go see if Traesa was all right. He had to come up with a better way to keep his eyes on her. Protect her.

The idea that had occurred to him earlier shot to the front of his mind. It would be the perfect solution. A marriage of convenience would be good for both of them. He could find a rental house in an area of town far from the boardinghouse and the Hilliard mansion. Traesa could come to the office with him every day. With her helping him search, they should be able to find the papers he needed to settle the estate much quicker.

~

Traesa had just seated a group of people at one of the longer tables when she noticed Wilson standing in the doorway of the dining room. Happiness at seeing him was quickly overshadowed by the memory of seeing her brother. She didn't want him to worry about her. Maybe Quinton wouldn't come here again. But could she count on that? *What a dilemma.*

"Mr. Pollard, where would you like to sit?" No matter how professional she tried to be, this time her words came out breathy.

"I'm not ready to be seated just yet. I'll be back in a few minutes."

He turned and headed toward Mrs. Kelley's office, and he looked as if something was on his mind. She started serving the diners, but her gaze often strayed toward the foyer. She had taken the food to four different tables before he came out the office door.

She met him at the entrance to the dining room. "Are you ready now?"

"Mrs. Kelly said you can take a break and eat with me. I'd like to sit as far from other people as we can. We have things to discuss."

She had never seen him burdened like that. Maybe she shouldn't bring up what happened earlier today. She didn't want to add to his problems. Since most of the people were leaving to go back to work, she quickly found a table that would fit their needs. He sat, but she continued to stand.

"I don't want to make someone else wait on us. I'll get our food." She took out her pencil and pad.

He stared up at her. "I don't care what you bring me. Just get what you like, and I'll have the same thing."

He had never been so short with her. Was she in some kind of trouble? She whirled around and almost ran toward the kitchen. She picked up a tray and put the closest things on it before returning to their table.

After Wilson said a prayer over their food, he raised his head and looked into her eyes. He didn't even take a bite. "Miss Kildare, I know what happened in the kitchen this morning."

"How could you know?" She took the napkin and folded it across her lap and started eating.

"From the man who chased Quinton." He still didn't take a bite. He must be really upset. "Remember I told you I had a guard outside the boardinghouse. That's who chased him."

Finally, he ate something, too. "The people in your family are my responsibility until we're able to settle the estate."

"So where is Quinton now?"

"We don't know. The guard lost him." He wiped his mouth with his napkin. "The security company has sent out a team to the wooded area where he escaped to try to find him."

"So what happens now?" She sipped her water and tried another bite.

He put his fork back down and leaned toward her. "That's why I wanted to talk to you privately. It's hard for me to protect you when we're not together. I have an idea that could be good for both of us. Some of the clients of the law firm don't think a younger single man can be a good lawyer. Two of them have already taken their business elsewhere. I did have a new client yesterday, but if more clients want to leave, it could ruin the firm."

He seemed to be rambling, and it didn't make sense to her. How did that affect her?

"If we were to marry, it would help both of us. You'd be safe because you could come to the office with me every day. And maybe the clients will trust me more." His questioning gaze never left her face.

Her thoughts scattered all over the place. How could he want to marry her when they had never been courting? And what about love? She wanted a marriage filled with love like the one her parents had.

She took a sip of water to moisten her parched throat, but it didn't do anything for the fluttering in her stomach. She liked Wilson. She really did, but marriage to him had never entered her thoughts. Actually, she had figured that she might never marry since she was no longer a member of the Hilliard family. No man had ever asked to court her like they did with Charlotte. And she really wanted to be courted, not just an arrangement for protection.

He picked up his water glass and took a long draught. Maybe his throat was as dry as hers was.

"I've heard of marriages of convenience that turned into

something wonderful," he said. "That's what I'm suggesting. That we get married to help each of us. But without expectations of...everything that...comes with marriage...until we are both ready for that."

She'd never seen him have to search for words before. And she didn't have an answer for him right now. How could he expect her to?

He started eating his food again, so she did too. As they ate, he asked her about her day and other inconsequential things as if he hadn't just astounded her with his idea.

After they ate dessert, he reached for her hand. "I'm not asking you for an answer now. Think about it, and I will too. But I hope it won't take too long for us to decide."

He left her at the door and strode out of the boarding house without looking back.

CHAPTER 11

*T*raesa stared at his receding back until he was out of her sight, her heart beating double time. She would have been happy if Wilson had asked to court her, but this was a different situation altogether. She couldn't decide how she felt about it. Happy? Sad? Disappointed? Elated? Indifferent?

Not indifferent, never that. She glanced around. At least, everyone had left the dining room. She'd always had a hard time hiding her emotions, and anyone around would be able to see she was upset. *Upset, that's what I feel.* Upset and confused.

Mrs. Kelley came through from the foyer and headed toward her table. "I'm looking for Mr. Pollard. I thought he was here with you."

Traesa swallowed her emotion and tried for a shaky smile. "You just missed him."

"Really?" The woman studied her face, making her more uncomfortable than before. "Are you all right?"

She gave a quick nod. "Yes." Sliding from her chair, she started stacking the dirty dishes on the table.

"You don't have to do that. He asked me to give you the rest of the day off." Her landlady reached for the stack. "I agreed."

"I don't need the time off now." She couldn't keep a slight tremble from her voice, so she cleared her throat. "I'd rather work, if that's all right with you."

Traesa didn't want to go to her room. She'd just get bogged down mulling over what Wilson had said. It would drive her insane. There was no way she could concentrate on finishing the book she was reading either.

Mrs. Kelley smiled at her. "It's fine with me, but you don't need to go to the kitchen again until Christine starts supper."

As she returned to her room, thoughts scrambled in her mind. Mrs. Kelley insisted on paying her, but it wasn't enough to live on even if she continued to stay in the boardinghouse as part of her wages. Was she destined to do menial labor the rest of her life? At least she wouldn't be out on the streets. She never wanted to be there again, and she'd thought coming west on the orphan train guaranteed she wouldn't.

Maybe Wilson's suggestion didn't sound so unreasonable. The love she'd seen between her parents, and the love Abuela had shared with her about the history of good marriages in her family, wasn't essential for living, was it? Of course, the dream of true love that had taken root in her heart when she was just a child still lingered. Maybe it was time to grow up and face reality. If she wasn't really adopted, as Quinton said, those dreams must be shut away in the back corner of her mind.

What if, sometime after they married, Wilson met someone he could really love? Would he resent her? Even get rid of her? Or she might meet someone she could share a deep love with.

So many complications had entered her life recently, they overcame her. Grief for the loss of her grandmother, finding out she might not have been adopted, and the horrible attack from Quinton. At least God had saved her from his evil intentions. Just allowing the thought of his attempted rape made her stomach revolt. She reached the chamber pot just in time to keep from making a big mess on the carpet. Sitting back on her heels, she wiped her mouth with the hanky from her sleeve.

After a few minutes of crying out to God in her heart, she arose and swished her mouth out with the water from her pitcher and bowl, then poured it into the chamber pot as well. Fear of Quinton remained in her thoughts as she paced the room. He knew where she was now. Would he come for her when no one was looking? She couldn't let that happen.

Marriage to Wilson, even a marriage of convenience with no love attached, would be better than always being on alert against Quinton. Wilson would protect her, and maybe Quinton would never find where they were when they lived somewhere else.

She glanced at the clock. It was time to go downstairs and help fix supper. At least she was learning to cook. That would come in handy when...if she married Wilson. Especially if he didn't want to come to the boardinghouse for meals.

$\sim$

Wilson tried to make headway through the files, but his conversation with Traesa distracted him often. What was she thinking? He hoped Mrs. Kelley giving her the afternoon off helped her as she considered his proposal.

He hadn't thought much about how he would propose to his future wife, but this situation had never entered his mind. It was the only way he could think of to protect Traesa...and the law firm. He hunted through the files all afternoon with no disturbances from clients, which wasn't a good thing.

Not wanting to arrive at supper during the rush, he continued to work and planned his arrival for when the dining room should be clearing out. That way, he could sit with Traesa without anyone close enough to hear them. It might be too soon for her to have an answer for him, but if it wasn't, he wanted their conversation to be completely private.

When he arrived at the dining room, he saw Traesa carrying a tray with filled plates to a couple sitting near the fireplace. He couldn't keep from frowning. So much for getting her the time off. He forced a smile and sat at an empty table near one of the potbelly stoves.

Empty tray in her hand, Traesa headed toward him. "You're later than usual, Mr. Pollard, and we've run out of some of the more popular items." She gripped the tray under one arm and reached for her pad in her pocket with her other hand. "What would you like to eat?"

He continued to watch her face, looking for signs of a decision. He didn't discern any. "Have you eaten?"

"Not yet."

She glanced out the window instead of looking at him. That wasn't a good sign.

"I don't know what you have left. Just bring me what you plan to eat, and we can dine together. All right?"

She answered with a nod. "Of course. I'll be right back."

He watched her make her way between the tables, her hips swaying slightly. She was an attractive woman, and he noticed a few other men watching her as well. Maybe she would agree with his idea. He wanted to protect her from more men than just Quinton. Probably, none of the ones in this room would hurt her, but the only way to be sure was for her to agree with his plan. He sat with one elbow poised on the table while he watched the kitchen doorway.

Traesa soon returned carrying their meals. On the way, she passed the last group of diners as they exited. *Good.* Now they would have all the privacy they needed for their important discussion. After placing the dishes on the table, she sat across from him and bowed her head while he said the blessing. When he looked up again, she was still looking down. He really wanted to study her when they talked so he could get some idea of what she was thinking before he approached the important subject again.

He took a bite of his food then laid his fork on the edge of his plate. "Did you have time to consider my proposal?"

She raised her head, and her eyes widened. "Is that what it was? A proposal?"

"I thought it was." He cleared his throat, which now felt as if no food could go past it.

"I've read novels with proposals, and none of them were like this one." After a pause, a soft smile crept across her lips then quickly disappeared. "Yes, I didn't come down to work until I needed to help the cook fix supper. I told Mrs. Kelley I wanted to work, instead of staying in my room all afternoon."

She glanced down at her plate long enough to eat a bite.

"So what did you think? Are you ready to give me some kind of an answer? If not, it's all right."

He held his breath waiting. She stared in his eyes as if she was trying to read his mind.

"I'm not sure how all this would work." She clasped her hands in her lap. "Do you know?"

He let out his breath. What did she want him to say? He had been thinking about little else all afternoon.

"I've considered several things." He leaned closer to her. "Maybe we could rent a small house for right now.. Maybe we could find one where Quinton wouldn't think to look for us."

"That might work. What else?" She sounded as if she might agree with him. "Where would we get married? And when?"

"I want the people who know about it to believe the marriage is real—"

"And I don't want to live a lie!"

He saw the flash of anger in her eyes before she shuttered it. "It won't be a lie. I'll marry you with the full intention of it being a real marriage in every sense of the word at some time. But until you…we are ready to consummate the relationship, there will still be a chance of having the marriage annulled if either one of us wants that."

She flinched at his words. He was only trying to let her know that she would have a way out if things didn't work, but he realized she would be terribly hurt if that happened. She wouldn't want an annulment any more than she would want a divorce. Both would put a stain on her reputation.

He never wanted to do that.

Her gaze dropped to her hands. "If this wedding is going to happen, when and where will it be without Quinton finding out about it."

"He'll find out if he reads the newspaper, because I'll put a notice in the paper so my clients will know." He couldn't tell what she thought about that. "If he doesn't know what your name was before your parents changed it, that won't be a problem."

"When the Hilliards took me home, they introduced me to the other children as Theresa Hilliard, so he wouldn't know my real name."

"That helps. Maybe we could have the pastor of our church marry us. I could ask Mrs. Kelley if we could get married here in the parlor."

She placed her hands beside her plate and raised her chin high. "What about my sisters? Can they attend?"

"If they know, it might put them and us in danger, especially if Quinton tries to come back to the mansion again."

~

*T*raesa hadn't thought of that. The things Wilson said made a lot of sense. He had a good heart, trying to protect so many people. And she didn't believe he wanted to hurt her.

"How soon do you think this will all happen?" She waited breathlessly for his answer.

He smiled at her, but she couldn't smile back. "As soon as I can get it all together. Hopefully, within a week. If you agree."

She let out her breath in a long sigh. "I agree."

But she didn't look at him as she said it. She arose and walked across the dining room then up to her room. Although she knew her feelings for Wilson could easily grow into love, he was so businesslike. Was it possible that his feelings for her could someday be love? It didn't seem so right now. With the door locked, she dropped onto the bed with her face buried into the pillow before the sobs began.

Her dreams of a marriage with true love floated away on her tears.

CHAPTER 12

*W*ilson hurried out of his boardinghouse. Traesa had actually agreed. He'd been so sure it would take more time to convince her that his plan was good. Both for her and for him. He hadn't anticipated having to move so quickly to get everything ready for the wedding. He wouldn't be able to spend as much time searching for the documents he needed to take care of the Hilliard estate. Good thing tomorrow was Saturday, and none of his clients would expect him to be in his office.

He decided to go over to the office right away so he could call Reverend Malone in privacy.

"Hello." His pastor answered after the first ring.

Thank goodness.

"This is Wilson Pollard."

"What can I do for you this evening?" When he'd arrived less than a month before, this new pastor had immediately immersed himself into the needs of the church members and community.

"Nothing tonight, but I wondered if you'd have time for me to come talk to you tomorrow. I shouldn't take too much time."

Pastor Malone laughed. "That's what I'm here for. To minister to people whenever needed. When do you want to come?"

After they set a time and hung up, Wilson stayed to continue his search.

When he arrived in the dining room the next morning for breakfast, he looked for Treasa. She didn't usually serve at breakfast, but he hoped she would be there. He saw when she stepped into the entrance from the other boardinghouse and hurried across the room.

"Traesa, would you join me?"

"Yes." Her answer sounded almost tentative. "Could we talk in the parlor before we have breakfast?"

He hoped she hadn't changed her mind. "Of course." He ushered her into the room and let her choose where to sit. After she settled in a wingback chair, he sat at the end of the couch nearest to her. They were far enough from the doorway, so their conversation would be private.

Probably, she had something to say to him she didn't want anyone else to hear. That could be good news...or not. *Lord, let it be good news.*

"Did you sleep well last night?" His plan hadn't been to upset her so much that she wouldn't.

Since he'd slept so well, that was what he wanted for her too. Her life since her grandmother died had been so hard on her. He hated that she couldn't leave the boardinghouse. She must feel like a prisoner, but he couldn't take a chance on Quinton finding her somewhere else. No telling what he would do if he did.

"Yes. I finished reading my book and went right to sleep." Her eyes were bright today, and she smiled at him.

"I'm glad. Are you working today?"

"I have the day off. What about you?"

"I actually have an appointment this morning with Reverend Malone."

Her eyes widened. "About the wedding?"

He took her hand in his. "If we're going to get married next weekend, I have a lot to do."

"Can I help?" She gently clasped her hands in her lap.

He couldn't tell if she was really interested or just being polite. "I'll take care of everything. I'll make an appointment on Monday to see a couple of houses for rent. I'd like you to go with me then."

She took a moment before she answered him. "Yes, I'd like to see the houses too. Before we move into one."

He flashed her a big smile. "I really want your opinion. You know they won't be anything like the Hilliard mansion."

She gazed out the window. "There are a lot of things you don't know about me." She took a deep breath. "Before my parents died, we lived in a tiny house. After they died, I had to live on the streets. It was hard."

Finally, she looked at him, studying his face. He tried to understand what that meant without seeming to condemn her. That was the last thing he wanted.

"You don't have to tell me any of the details if you don't want to."

"I want you to understand." A heavy sigh seeped from between her lips. "I try not to think about it. Several other orphans became my friends. We helped each other as much as we could. Finding food. Finding clothing. Finding a place to sleep each night. For four years. It felt like an eternity."

He leaned toward her. "Traesa, I'm so sorry you had to go through all that." What else could he say to make her feel better?

"There's more. The trip on the orphan train was long. So many stops, and no one wanted a tall, skinny, Irish girl with kinky, flyaway curls and freckles all over her face." Tears slipped down her cheeks, and she wiped them away with both hands.

"You are not that girl now. You're a beautiful woman."

She glanced up, eyes wide. "Do you really...?"

He waited, hoping she'd finish her question. Wishing she were comfortable enough with him to ask whatever was on her mind.

She didn't.

"I know we'll find something much better than you dealt with when you were on the street."

"Mr. Pollard, I was the last child left standing on the stage of the church here in Fort Worth. Rejection and despair overwhelmed me. Then Mr. and Mrs. Hilliard showed up and claimed me. Said they wanted to adopt me."

His heart was breaking for the lost, lonely little girl. "I'm glad they did."

"But did they?" She paused. "According to Quinton, they didn't."

"We can't trust what Quinton says. That's why I'm trying so hard to find the original documents."

"When they took me home to their mansion, I felt like it was heaven. I'd never seen anything like it before. Suddenly, I had three sisters and a brother. And a grandmother. Both of my grandmothers died before I was born. I loved it when we went out to the ranch. I learned to ride a horse. We had so much room to roam, my new siblings and me. Now, I've lost my second set of parents and the only grandmother I've ever known. And my brother, though he was never that to me, not really. But my sisters... Everything's fallen apart."

Wilson wanted to take her in his arms and comfort her, but he didn't want to give her expectations he might not ever be able fulfill. He really hoped they would learn to love each other, but it might not happen. She had already been hurt by far too many people and too difficult circumstances.

He glanced at his timepiece and stood. "I have to go if I'm going to meet the pastor on time."

All the way to the church, he tried to decide just how much he should tell the man. Of course, ministers were like lawyers. Everything shared with them was shared in confidence.

Reverend Malone must have been watching for him because he came out of the parsonage before Wilson dismounted. He tied the reins to the hitching rail in front of the house.

"Do you want to come in for a cup of coffee, or would you rather go over to the church? Mrs. Malone has a pot on the stove for you."

"Thank her, but I just finished breakfast at my boardinghouse."

They walked next door together, and the pastor unlocked the door.

Good. Evidently no one else was in the building. Wilson didn't want anyone to know what was going on. He had never been in the pastor's office before. A sofa had been pushed against the wall across from the desk, which had two straight-backed chairs facing the pastor's leather one. A side table with a lamp sat at one end, a Bible resting near the light.

Reverend Malone gestured toward the sofa. "Let's sit here."

Wilson sat while the pastor lit the lamp. Sunshine streamed through the window, shining on the side of the room containing the desk and the bookcases. The man must be very educated to have that many volumes.

"Let's pray first." Reverend Malone bowed his head. "Dear heavenly Father. We ask you to be with Mr. Pollard and me as we discuss whatever he needs help with. Give me wisdom and guide our conversation as we seek to do Your will in our lives. In Jesus' name. Amen."

Wilson had nothing but respect for a man who sought God for guidance in everything. "I have a complicated situation to deal with."

"I hope I can be of help to you." The reverend leaned back and relaxed.

Wilson explained the situation, leaving nothing out. Telling him why he wanted to marry Traesa so quickly.

When he finished, Reverend Malone closed his eyes and looked as though he might be praying. He sat that way for several minutes while Wilson glanced around the room, noticing the homey touches. Mrs. Malone had probably wanted to make her husband's office comfortable and familiar. Framed photographs were nestled among the books, facing the pastor's desk. A crocheted doily covered the table under the lamp, and another one decorated the middle of the sofa back.

For a moment, he thought about his own office. Since Mr. Harrison had never married and Wilson was still a bachelor, no feminine touches warmed the room. Even though he had a nice place, it didn't feel as warm and welcoming as this one. Maybe after they were married, Traesa could help him remedy that.

"Let me get this straight." Reverend Malone's words pulled him from his thoughts. "You want to marry this woman to protect her. And for now, it will be a marriage of convenience. Does she want to marry you?"

"She has agreed."

"And you want to make covenant vows before God for this kind of marriage?" The pastor's question made it sound wrong.

"I will be making vows before God that I intend to keep. I believe the marriage will become a real union eventually. I've heard of many successful and loving couples who started this way."

"Does she feel the same way you do?"

"I think so."

"You don't *know* so?"

"I'm not prepared to say that." He cringed as each word came out of his mouth.

"I will need to meet with both of you before I will agree to conduct the ceremony. When can you bring her?"

He wasn't surprised. "Can we meet with you sometime on

Monday?" He could bring her with him when they went to look at houses.

"Why not tomorrow after the service?"

Wilson stared at the ceiling and huffed out a breath. "She's still in mourning, and she hasn't been attending church yet."

"I knew I hadn't seen her. Do you think she's in danger in church?" The man kept pushing.

Wilson leaned forward. "I can keep her safer by bringing her on Monday. That way not as many people will see her. Could we do that?"

"As you wish, but I will need to be able to talk to her in private before I give you my answer." Reverend Malone stood. "Come at ten o'clock."

As he walked out the door, Wilson mulled over everything his pastor said. He needed to spend quite a lot more time in prayer this weekend. So far God hadn't put a check in his spirit about the plan.

CHAPTER 13

Traesa waited for Wilson in the parlor at nine-thirty on Monday. They were going to see Reverend Malone because the pastor had requested it. What in the world did he want talk to her about?

Wilson hadn't told her what he and Reverend Malone had discussed on Saturday other than about the pastor marrying them. Did he tell him about the circumstances? She hoped not all of them. At breakfast all he talked about was taking her to see two houses they might rent. He didn't mention this meeting until he'd left her at the bottom of the stairs in the women's boardinghouse.

She had only met the minister at her grandmother's funeral. He didn't know her very well, and she didn't know him either. Her grief had been so strong that she hardly remembered anything that had taken place that day. Abuela's death had shaken the very foundation of her life. So many things had changed since then. The pain of her losses was too new, too harsh. For the first two weeks, the anguish in her heart stole her breath. Even now, she tried to keep from thinking about that time because her grief was still so fresh.

She pulled her hanky from the sleeve of her dress and patted her cheeks to stop the tears that even now seeped from her eyes. She would be a mess by the time they arrived at the pastor's office. Dropping into the comfortable wingback chair, she slid out of her cape. Even though the late May morning was still a little too cool outside without the wrap, the parlor was comfortably warm. She leaned her elbows on the arms of the chair and dropped her face in her hands.

"Traesa, dear, are you all right?" Mrs. Kelley's sweet voice penetrated her thoughts.

She glanced up and tried to smile. "Yes." Her answer sounded weak even in her own ears.

Mrs. Kelley sat in the matching chair. "I know you're still mourning the passing of your grandmother. It hasn't been but a few weeks. It's okay to cry sometimes. That helps relieve the pain. I know. Even though it's been more than five years, I still cry over the loss of my husband every once in a while."

Once again, tears filled Traesa's eyes. As she sopped them up, her handkerchief became saturated.

Mrs. Kelley pulled a clean white square of soft cotton from her pocket and pressed it into Traesa's hand. "Take this, and let me have the other one. I'll put it in the laundry."

After she left, Traesa thanked God that He had put her in this place where everyone took such good care of her. They couldn't take the place of what she'd lost, but at least she wasn't alone in her grief.

Hearing the outside door to the foyer open and close, she looked up.

Wilson hurried toward her. "Traesa, sorry I'm late. A phone call from a possible new client took longer than I thought it would."

She stood, and he picked up her cape. He had her turn around before he wrapped the garment over her shoulders. She felt like a butterfly cocooned in warmth. When would she break through her chrysalis and leave the darkness of her sorrow?

He opened the door. She expected to see a hansom cab in the street in front of the house. Instead, a horse and an open surrey waited. The black buggy had fringe around the roof. She stopped and stared.

"It's such a pretty day I decided to rent something from the livery."

Wilson took her hand and led her to the waiting conveyance. He helped her into the seat before going around the front toward his side. He stopped and pulled a carrot from his pocket and offered it to the waiting horse.

After stepping into the surrey and picking up the reins to start them moving down the street, he turned toward her. "When we move into the house, I'll want to get some kind of carriage or buggy. I thought we could try out some to see which one we like best."

Surprised, she didn't know what to say. She finally managed, "That sounds like a good idea."

He turned the buggy toward the church, and they arrived right at ten o'clock. After tying the reins to the hitching rail near the office, he hurriedly helped her down. They met Reverend Malone coming toward the door as they entered.

"Hello, Reverend." Wilson held out his hand.

The minister shook it briefly. "I saw you pull up. That's why I came out of my office to meet you." He turned toward Traesa. "It's good to see you again, Miss Hilliard."

Evidently, Wilson hadn't told the man about her name change. She hoped that wouldn't be a problem.

In the office, Reverend Malone had her sit beside Wilson on the sofa while he pulled a chair close to them. He went over what Wilson had told him on Saturday. The man never mentioned her changed name, but he knew about Quinton and his actions and claims. That would make it easier for her to talk to him.

He gazed at her a moment. "Is this what you understand about what is happening?"

She nodded. "That's right."

He turned toward Wilson. "I'd like to ask you to wait outside in the hallway, far enough away that you can't hear what we're talking about, if you would."

Wilson turned to her, eyebrows lifted, and she gave him a slight nod. When he went out of the room, the pastor left the door open. She turned her attention back toward the man of God.

"Is he forcing you to agree with him? Do you want to make covenant vows before God in this matter? You can trust me, Miss Hilliard. I only have your best in mind."

She discerned nothing but honest concern. "Mr. Pollard and I have discussed this matter at great length, and I agree it's the best way for us to proceed. I understand all the ramifications of what we're doing."

"All right. If you're sure."

"There's one thing Wilson might not have mentioned."

A look of interest crossed his face, and he steepled his fingers. "And what is that?"

"Since there's a good chance I wasn't adopted, I've gone back to my original name." She twisted her hands in her lap. "I'm Traesa Kildare, not Theresa Hilliard. That's the name I want to use for the wedding. I pray that we will reach a time when we will truly love each other."

~

*W*ilson could hear the murmur of their voices, but he stayed far enough away that he couldn't understand the words. He paced across the vestibule and wondered what was so important that he couldn't hear what was being said. Not too many minutes had passed before the pastor headed toward him.

"You can join us now." The man turned back toward his office.

Wilson wasn't far behind. As he arrived at the open doorway, he glanced at Traesa. She sat with a small Mona Lisa-like smile on her face. Evidently everything was all right.

Reverend Malone gestured for him to be seated again before he perched on the hard seat of the ladder-back chair. They discussed the day, time, and location they were aiming for. Of course, it was Wilson's job to make sure it would all work out the way they planned. He was pretty sure he could handle that.

When they left the church, they headed toward the neighborhood where the first house they were going to look at was located. Wilson didn't even want to point out the cottage to Traesa. This neighborhood looked seedy, and the one with the house number he sought was the worst on the block. He glanced at her, and she was frowning too.

He stopped at the end of the block. "I had no idea the house was in this kind of neighborhood. I would never choose any of these for our first home."

Her frown disappeared, but no smile replaced it. "I've seen worse."

He took her hand in his. "I want our marriage to work, and I want to provide the best I can afford for you. This area doesn't even come close to that."

Finally, her lips tipped up at the corners. "Thank you, Mr. Pollard."

He laughed. "You really need to start calling me Wilson."

"Thank you, Wilson. I'll try to remember." Her eyes twinkled.

The other house on his list was several streets over, and the neighborhood was far better than the one they left behind. He stopped the buggy in front of a cottage at least twice its size.

It was a white house with dark blue shutters and a matching front door. It sat on a lovely little plot of land dotted with bushes and surrounded by a white picket fence.

A happy sigh escaped from Traesa's mouth. "Oh, Wilson, it's lovely."

"I have the key. Shall we check the inside?"

He jumped down and hurried around to lift her from the conveyance.

After he opened the gate, they crossed the stepping stones toward the small porch with the arched roof.

She stopped before mounting the stairs. "Look at these flower beds. Someone has taken good care of this place. I look forward to the flowers blooming. They're covered with buds."

He glanced at her. "Do you like to garden?"

"My mother taught me how to raise flowers before she died. The Hilliards have a gardener, so I haven't done any gardening there, but I remember much of what Máthair and I did back then."

He led the way to the front door and opened it. Bright spring sunlight poured through the many windows illuminating all the rooms they could see.

"Oh." She glanced around the parlor. It reminded her of the one at the boardinghouse. Every table glistened, and the sofa and upholstered chairs looked almost new. Enough lamps to light up the room at night were scattered among the various pieces of furniture.

"Everything is so beautiful." She ran her fingers across the back of one of the chairs. "Does all the furniture stay here?"

"If we want it to." He looked at the paper with all the particulars Mr. MacTavish, the banker handling the rentals, had given him. "A local couple had this built for one of their mothers. After living here for about a year, she went to visit another of her children. While she was there, she became ill and died. They decided to keep the house and rent it out. If the renter needs furniture, a deal can be made that way. If not, the contents will be removed."

Traesa crossed the entrance hall to the other front room. "This is a library with a nice desk in it. Look at all those books. If we rent this one, it just might become my favorite room." She approached the wall of bookshelves and glanced at the titles. "I haven't read a lot of these, and they look interesting."

He followed her as she wandered through the rest of the house. Two bedrooms, a dining room, a kitchen, and a bathing room. Everything was pristine. He decided this was the place for their first home, if Traesa agreed.

"What do you think?"

"I love it." She clasped her hands against her chest. "When we get married, we can move right in. This is wonderful."

He agreed. Now he needed to take care of setting up the wedding this coming weekend. When he took her back to the boardinghouse, he planned to talk to Mary Kelley about having the ceremony in the parlor there. If she agreed, everything else should fall into place.

CHAPTER 14

*T*oday was their wedding day. Traesa sat in the chair beside her window and watched dawn creep across the horizon. She had gone to sleep the night before but quickly awakened again. Thoughts of her imminent wedding captured her attention.

The unknown loomed before her. How did a marriage of convenience really work? As far as she knew, none of her acquaintances were in that kind of relationship. Or if they were, they didn't want anyone else to know. So many times in her life she'd been in these circumstances where everything she knew changed in what felt like a whirlwind. Her future was only a blur in her imagination. Her stomach fluttered as if she were in a tornado, twisting and turning without knowing the direction she would go next. She gazed up at the ceiling.

"Lord, please help me understand what is really going on. Am I in Your will, or not?" She bowed her head and waited. Soon a sense of peace hovered over her. Maybe what they were doing was all right with God.

She knew Wilson only had her best interest in mind.

Keeping her safe was important to him. He'd exhibited that over and over. What more could she ask for?

Before the day was over on Monday, he had rented the house she loved, and they had taken most of her possessions there during the week. She looked at the blue enameled Chatelaine watch Abuela had given her for her nineteenth birthday. It hung from a brooch she often wore.

Seven o'clock. The wedding was scheduled for ten o'clock this Saturday morning. In a little over three hours, she would become Mrs. Wilson Pollard. Another major change in her life. And she didn't know what to expect from this one.

"Traesa." A light tap on her door drew her attention.

She hurried over to open it.

Sheila stood in the hallway with a tray in her hands. "Mrs. Sanders thought you might like to have your breakfast in your room."

She stepped back so her friend could enter.

Sheila set the tray on the table by the window. "Aren't you excited?"

Am I? Of course, she was. And apprehensive. She glanced down at the food. There was quite a lot of it.

"Would you join me?" She gestured toward the tray.

"I was hoping you'd say that. Mrs. Sanders suggested you might like company this morning, since you don't have any family with you." Sheila handed her one of the plates and took the other one. "You get what you want to eat, and I'll eat the rest."

After they filled their plates, Traesa sat on the edge of the bed so Sheila could sit in the chair as they ate. "I wasn't sure whether I would go down for breakfast. Now that the food is here, I realize I'm hungry. I'm not sure what the plans are for after the wedding, so I probably should eat now."

Sheila noticed the two dresses she had hung on the wall

hooks on either side of her washbowl and pitcher. "Which one are you going to wear?"

Traesa stared at both of them—her favorites. The emerald green looked more like a traveling suit, even though it wasn't two pieces. Abuela had loved to dress her in green. She said it complimented her coloring. The second dress was watered silk that changed from green to blue according to the light. It had a softer shape with layers of fabric draped around the bodice and skirt. She had only worn it once.

"I haven't made up my mind yet."

As they were finishing the food, another knock sounded on the door.

"I'll get it." Sheila hurried to accomplish that. "Bridgett, I hadn't seen you yet today."

The other woman addressed Traesa. "There's someone here to see you. Should I bring her up?"

Her? Who in the world could it be? Not one of her sisters. "Who is it?"

"Mrs. Richards, and she has several packages with her."

Traesa stood. "Bring her up."

When Bridgett left, she set her plate on the tray. "I'm finished if you want to take the tray back to the kitchen. Thank you so much for thinking of me."

The cook's helper headed out as Bridgett and Mrs. Richards arrived at the top of the front stairs. Traesa went to meet them.

Mrs. Richards set the packages on the floor and wrapped her arms around Traesa. It was the best hug she'd experienced since Abuela passed away. She relished the warmth of the embrace. By the time they finished, Bridgett had taken all the packages into Traesa's room.

"I'll let you enjoy your guest," she said as she passed them going back downstairs.

When they were in her room, Traesa shut the door.

The housekeeper stood back. "Let me look at you. I've missed you so much. You've been an important part of the Hilliard household for so long. It's not the same since you've been gone."

"I miss all of you too."

Mrs. Richards started opening her packages. "I've brought Mrs. Hilliard's wedding dress. She told me once that she hoped you'd want to wear it. Charlotte was too tall to use it, and the other girls will be too. This was her grandmother's."

She pulled a dress from a carpetbag and unfolded it on the bed.

Treasa's eyes watered. Abuela hadn't said anything to her about wanting her to wear this dress. She'd never seen it. It was blue silk with short sleeves and a blue silk band at the empire waist. Fine lace covered all but the band.

It was gorgeous. Oh, she hoped it would fit her. Imagine, her great-great-grandmother's wedding dress. What a wonderful heirloom. Next came a white lace *mantilla* and a gold comb set with pearls that would anchor the veil to her hairstyle.

"I've never seen anything so beautiful." Traesa had a hard time getting the words past the tears gathering in her throat.

"I brought new unmentionables and slippers. Now you'll have something old, something new, something borrowed, and something blue." Mrs. Richards laid each thing on the bed beside the dress. "And I have a penny for your shoe. I know it's superstitious, but I hope the items will bring blessings on your marriage."

Traesa had not imagined something like this happening to her since she was run out of the house by her former brother.

~

Wilson arrived half an hour before the ceremony.

Mrs. Kelley met him in the foyer. "I need some help with the furniture."

At least, he'd have something to do to keep him busy. Even though he was eager for the coming event, he was also nervous. He'd never thought of getting married this way. "That's why I arrived early, in case you needed me."

They moved all the furniture in the parlor against the walls.

"Would you serve as a witness to the ceremony?" He smiled at her.

"Yes." She cleared her throat. "Would it be presumptive of me to ask if we could put some of the chairs from the dining room in here so the people who have worked with Traesa can attend, too?"

Why didn't I think of that? "That's a good idea. Who all will it be?"

"Bridgett, Molly, Sheila, and Mrs. Sanders want to come. So do Pat and I."

He headed toward the dining room. "I'll bring in ten chairs. Mrs. Richards will want to sit down after she accompanies Traesa and takes the place of a father who would give her away."

When the last chair was in place, Reverend Malone entered the foyer. Behind him, his wife was carrying a small bouquet.

She handed the flowers to Mrs. Kelley. "I wanted the bride to have these. A wedding is so much more festive with flowers." She sat in one of the chairs.

Mrs. Kelly gathered all the boardinghouse attendees and brought them to the parlor, then she went up the stairs with the bouquet. When she returned, Traesa and Mrs. Richards followed her down the stairs. The pastor and Wilson stood in front of the assembled friends.

As the two women approached, Wilson gazed at his bride. A vision of loveliness.

Her eyes met his, and her hands started trembling, causing the bouquet to sway. She glanced down at the carpet, and he wondered what she was thinking. Did she have doubts? Was she wishing they had found another way to keep her safe?

"Dearly beloved, we are gathered here…" Reverend Malone started the ceremony in the usual way.

Each word became like a weighted stone, sinking into him. In a very few moments, he'd speak sacred vows, and he'd mean every word. Vows that would change the rest of his life and Traesa's. What if he'd made the wrong decision?

His pastor turned toward him. "Wilson, repeat after me. I, Wilson Pollard, take thee, Traesa Kildare, to be my wedded wife."

He swallowed the lump in his throat and spoke the words.

"To have and to hold from this day forward." The pastor's voice was strong.

Wilson wished he had something to drink so his mouth wouldn't be so dry. He realized he was gripping Traesa's hands too hard. He loosened his hold a little as he repeated the words.

When it was her turn to repeat vows, Wilson noticed the word "obey" added to hers. He only remembered attending one wedding before. And he hadn't paid that much attention to the words of promise.

All the time he'd known Traesa, he hadn't spent so much of it looking straight at her face. Her eyes had several shades of green speckled with tiny golden sparks. Her mouth looked like Cupid's bow. *Where did that thought come from?* He'd probably heard it somewhere.

As she almost whispered the final words of her vows, his heart hitched. What if he had destroyed her chance for a marriage filled with love? He hoped theirs would turn into one, but what if it didn't?

The trust shining from her face made his responsibility feel much heavier. He would have to figure out how to be a good husband.

Mrs. Kelley and Mrs. Crawford followed them out of the parlor. They stepped in front of the couple, stopping their progress toward the front door. *What do they want?*

"We have a wedding cake and fruit punch for everyone in the dining room."

Mrs. Crawford gestured toward the table he hadn't noticed when he gathered the chairs from the other side of the room. He took his wife's hand and led her toward it.

"Oh, look, Wilson. How beautiful."

Her soft words probably reached only his ears. Tears glistened in her eyes. She wiped them away with her other hand.

"I never expected anything like this."

Neither had he.

The other wedding attendees followed behind them, chattering away about the beautiful ceremony and the beautiful bride. *She is indeed. And she's now my wife.*

He would be responsible for her for the rest of their lives.

~

*A*fter the unexpected reception was over, Traesa, accompanied by Mrs. Richards, went upstairs. "Will you take the wedding things back to the mansion for me?"

The older woman studied her face for a moment. "Are you sure you want me to do that? Your grandmother wanted you to keep it. After you've changed into what you want to wear the rest of the day, I'll pack it the way I brought it to you. Then you can take it to your home and store it."

Traesa hadn't thought of doing that. "Okay." Maybe some day, if their marriage actually became a real one, she would have a daughter who would wear these clothes from her great-great-great-grandmother. Traesa could tell her daughter the stories Abuela had shared with her. Nothing could take away the strong bonds of love, even if she hadn't been adopted.

Mrs. Richards undid the row of buttons down the back of the dress from the neckline to her hips. "I'm not sure when I'll be able to see you again. My love goes with you, and I'll be praying for you and Mr. Pollard every day. That's what your grandmother would have done. I'm hoping the time will come soon when we can be together."

The words soothed Traesa's heart, and she almost felt as if Abuela were there with them.

CHAPTER 15

JUNE

*T*raesa woke and went to her washstand, where she poured water from the pitcher into the bowl. This set with roses painted on the side of both vessels was a wedding gift from the kitchen staff at the boardinghouse. She missed all her friends from there, but she loved having a home of her own.

She leaned over the bowl and started her ablutions. The cool water on her face helped her wake up completely. After drying her face with the soft towel hanging on the rack attached to the side of the washstand, she went to choose what to wear.

Her thoughts returned to all the wonderful things that had happened since they married. The day after the wedding, she and Wilson attended a small church near the cottage. People welcomed them with open arms, making her feel right at home. She was experiencing a whole new life to go along with her marriage.

The pastor stood on the top step outside the door as each person left the sanctuary.

"Good sermon, Reverend Stewart." Wilson held out his hand, and the minister shook it.

"Glad to welcome you. Hope you'll come back. Are you new to Fort Worth?"

Wilson shook his head. "We've lived here, but we got married yesterday and are new to this neighborhood."

A petite woman with blond hair in the new Gibson Girl style approached. A feather in the blue hat perched on top waved in the gentle breeze. "Henry." She slipped her hand around her husband's arm. "Let's invite this new couple to have dinner with us."

"Of course, my dear." Turning toward Wilson, he extended the invitation, ending with, "We'd like to get to know you."

The meal had been delicious. When they started home, Traesa hoped she and Mrs. Stewart would become good friends.

The weeks of going to work with Wilson had proved to be satisfying. She helped him as they continued to search for the missing papers. As they finished with each crate, she alphabetized the files so he would be able to find them more easily when he needed them again.

In the evenings, she was thankful for all the things Mrs. Sanders had taught her to cook while she worked at the boardinghouse. Wilson always complimented the meals. However, she knew she would soon run out of ideas. Maybe she could find a book of receipts when they went into town again.

After checking how she looked in the standing Cheval mirror, she headed out of her bedroom.

Wilson was talking on the phone. "I don't usually meet with clients on the weekend."

His words caught her attention.

She waited until he hung the earpiece in the hook on the side of the wooden instrument attached to the wall. "What was that about?"

He shook his head. "I've never had this happen before. A

man from out of town needs to see me, and he'll only be here today and tomorrow. I don't want us to miss church, so I'll meet with him today. It needs to be a private meeting, so I called the security firm to send a couple of guards to watch the house, just in case."

"Do you think that's really necessary?" She filled the coffee percolator and set it near the back of the hot side of the kitchen stovetop. As usual, Wilson had thoughtfully started the fire in the wood cookstove. "Quinton wouldn't think to look here for me."

"I'm not sure about anything to do with him." He pulled out a chair from the kitchen table and sat. "I'm just not willing to take a chance. If you want to go shopping later today, I'll go with you."

"We still have some of the food from the last time we went shopping. I have plenty to cook, so we won't need to go today." She pulled out a cast-iron skillet and set it in front of the coffee. "Would you like hotcakes for breakfast? We still have some ham, too."

After she filled two plates with their breakfast, she poured the coffee. Then she joined him at the table.

He bowed his head, and she did too. "Dear Lord, we thank you for this food and the hands that prepared it. Please be with each of us while we are apart today. Protect and keep us until we are together again. Amen."

After they had taken a few bites, she decided to approach him about the packed crates still in his bedroom and the living room. He should have unpacked them in the last few weeks, but he had been so busy.

"Wilson, I have unpacked everything that was brought here from the mansion, but many of your things aren't unpacked yet. Would you like me to do that while you're gone today?"

"That would be nice."

He seemed to be distracted, but that wasn't going to keep her from doing it. She couldn't rearrange anything in the living room until the crates were gone.

He took the last bite from his plate and stood. "That was delicious. Your hot cakes are the best I've ever tasted."

"Thank you." She warmed at the compliment.

After calling the security firm, he picked up his satchel and headed toward the front door. After he took his hat from the hall tree, he turned back toward her. "I don't like leaving you alone, but I'll be back as soon as I can."

After the door closed behind him, Traesa returned to the kitchen to do the dishes. She'd finish as quickly as she could. Hopefully, she'd be able to complete unpacking his crates before he returned.

~

*W*hen Wilson arrived at his office, two men waited in a buggy parked in front. Both were strangers. He wondered if the older man or the younger man was the one who'd called him. He tied his horse's reins to the hitching post and went to unlock the door.

Both men descended from the buggy and followed him inside. The younger one looked all around as if inspecting the building. *What is that all about?*

He shook hands with the men, welcoming them, then went behind his desk to sit in his office chair, which was more comfortable than the straight-backed ones on the other side of the desk.

"Please, gentlemen. Have a seat." He gestured to the two in front of him.

The older man quickly sat down as if he couldn't stand any longer.

The younger stayed standing. "I'm Carl Johnson. I called you because Mr. Harrison was my uncle. I'm his heir. Mr. Caldwell here was my uncle's lawyer. "I had moved to Alaska before my uncle died, and Mr. Caldwell has been trying to find me. We didn't move back to Iowa until two weeks ago. That's when I found out about my uncle's passing."

All kind of scenarios went through Wilson's mind. Why were the men in his office? Did Carl inherit the law firm? If so, where would that leave him? Hadn't there been enough turmoil in his life already? And now he just got married. He hoped whatever they wanted wouldn't affect his livelihood.

"How can I help you?"

Mr. Caldwell leaned forward. "I retired from reading the law a couple of years before Harrison died, so I don't have an office. I have Harrison's will, and I need to read part of it to Mr. Caldwell with you present. I felt that meeting at your office would work better than anywhere else, since you are also mentioned in the will and a junior partner in the firm."

The older man opened his satchel and pulled out a sheaf of papers and straightened them on the front edge of the desk. "Please, have a seat, Carl, so I don't have to look up at you."

Wilson leaned his forearms on his desk and watched as the man flipped through page after page of the document. It took quite a while for the other lawyer to get to the part where he was mentioned. In the meantime, he fidgeted, worrying about what changes he'd have to make in his working life, too.

Finally, Cadwell stopped shuffling pages. "In the event that you, Carl Johnson, decide that you don't want to read the law here in Fort Worth, Texas, you may sell the firm. It must be offered to Wilson Pollard first. If he wants to keep the firm, you may sell it to him for the sum of $500. If he doesn't have the whole $500 to pay you, you must allow him to pay it out in whatever terms he can afford."

The older man turned to Carl. "I'm assuming you'll want to keep the firm, with Mr. Pollard being a junior partner, as he was the last year with your uncle. Am I right?"

Johnson looked as surprised as Wilson felt. He stared into the distance as if he were far, far away. Silence grew heavy in the room before anyone spoke again.

Wilson was glad he'd been frugal and put most of the money he made in the bank. At least he and Traesa would have something to live off of in this transition time if it didn't last too long.

By the time the men finished their meeting, Carl Johnson was Wilson's new partner and the majority owner of the law firm. Wilson hoped they would be compatible.

Carl said, "I think we can work well together. You'll have to help me a lot. Because my uncle had wanted me to be a lawyer like he was, he sent me law books for presents. But even though I read a lot of them, I didn't take the time to really absorb them. I never thought I'd need to remember what I read, and I'm not familiar with Texas law."

"When do you want to start working here?"

"I'm going back home to see my family and talk to my wife. I may wait to move them here until I'm sure this is what I want to keep on doing. I'll be back hopefully in less than a week."

～

*W*hen Traesa finished cleaning the kitchen, she hurried into the living room. She wanted to unpack these crates before she did the ones in Wilson's bedroom. It took an hour to do the first ones. When everything was put in a proper place, she set those crates out on the back porch.

Back in the bedroom, she started on the other crates. The ones that contained some of his clothes were easy to empty. She did feel a little strange handling his unmentionables. She had helped her mother with the laundry when she was a child and dealt with her father's clothes. This was different. These belonged to her husband, who really wasn't her husband in every way. They were too personal.

Yes, she hoped their marriage would become more than it was now. But she didn't know how long that would take. Later today, after Wilson came home, she'd need to wash all the clothes they both had worn.

One crate contained other personal things. Handkerchiefs, belts, socks, cuff links. She put them in a neat order in the top drawer of his chest of drawers. While she was doing this, she noticed something already stuck in the back corner of the top drawer, a small bundle of greeting cards. She loved the colorful drawings on the fronts and the lovely verses usually found inside. Why had he kept them in his bureau drawer?

She untied the cord around them and opened the first one to read the verse, surprised to find a personal note as well. She read it out loud. "Dear Wilson, we miss you so much. Another year without you coming home has been hard. We do appreciate each Christmas and birthday card, but they aren't enough. Won't you please try to come soon? Or at least answer one of our letters? Love, Mother."

What did that mean? Surely he cared about his family. After the years without hers, she couldn't understand anyone not keeping in touch with his family. She'd have to ask Wilson about it when he got home. She finished emptying the last crate and taking it to the back porch, then she heard Wilson unlock the front door. She hurried into the living room to meet him.

"Welcome home, Wilson."

He shot her a quick smile, but something must be troubling him. She'd never seen that worried expression on his face. His brows were knitted tight, and the muscles in his jaws twitched.

"Traesa." He nodded at her.

He walked past her and into his bedroom, then shut the door. How could she ask him now about what she'd found? She didn't want to add to whatever burden he was carrying.

She went into the kitchen, fixed another pot of coffee, and set it on the stove. Maybe he'd come out by the time it finished percolating.

Sitting at the table, she folded her hands and bowed her head. *Dear Lord, please comfort my husband. Lift the burden from his heart.*

CHAPTER 16

*W*ilson shouldn't have practically ignored Traesa when he came home, but he needed to ponder what happened that morning. How would it affect Traesa and their marriage?

He had known there probably was an heir somewhere, but since Mr. Harrison used a different lawyer to draw up his will, Wilson had never seen it and had no way of knowing what it contained. It had been so long since the older lawyer died that Wilson had put away thoughts about the possibility of an heir. Four years was a long time.

Now, out of the clear blue, this man appeared and would be the senior partner. That would make Wilson the junior partner, again. Would his salary as junior partner be enough for Traesa and him? He didn't think the firm could support two families.

Wilson had to show Carl Johnson the ropes and catch him up with the various clients. He'd start with most of the clients that Mr. Harrison took care of. All except for the Hilliard family. Of course, he had gained several clients for the firm during the four years since Mr. Harrison had been gone. They should remain his, but a senior partner could change that.

While Wilson shed his suit, he mentally scanned the list of people his new partner needed to meet first.

Heaviness slowed his movements. He had enough to deal with without this new wrinkle. Having to protect Traesa from her wayward brother was a constant drain on his mental and emotional resources.

When he finished dressing in more casual clothes, he opened the top drawer of his bureau to look for his handkerchiefs. There they were right beside the bundle of greeting cards from his mother, which had been in the back corner of the drawer. Why were they at the front now?

Something about the bundle bothered him. It didn't look right. The cord wasn't tied the way he had it. Had Traesa snooped in his private papers? Surely not.

He undid the cord and looked through them. They were out of order.

She has no right.

Anger rose within him. He put them in order and tied them back together. After shoving an older handkerchief in his back pocket, he grabbed the doorknob and pulled the door open so fast it hit the wall.

Traesa was in the kitchen cooking dinner. At the harsh sound, her head swiveled, and she looked straight at him, her eyes wide and her hands shaking.

"What happened, Wilson?" She grabbed the towel from the countertop and dried her hands.

Counting to ten, he stared at her. The time wasn't enough to take away his anger. "Why were you snooping in my private papers?" Without him meaning to, his voice rose in volume with each word.

Her eyes widened even more, and he caught a flash of fear in her eyes.

He didn't want to scare her, but she needed to know what she could and could not do. "You had no right going through the cards from my mother." He modulated his tone a little lower. "Did you read what she wrote to me?"

With a small nod, she took a deep breath then cleared her throat. "I didn't mean any harm. You had said I could unpack your things."

He stomped across the room and stood before her. "Don't you know what is appropriate and what isn't?"

"Yes, I do." She tucked her hands into the pockets of her apron. "I only wanted to look at the pretty cards. They're beautiful."

"But you did more than that, didn't you? The messages were private between my mother and me."

Even though he towered above her petite stature, she stood her ground. "I did, and I don't understand them. How can someone who has a perfectly fine family not keep in contact with them?"

"It's none of your business." The words spewed like venom, even though she wasn't the reason he was in this terrible mood.

She crossed her arms. Tears hung on her eyelashes, but she kept her head high. "You've always had a family and a home. I haven't. Things have been hard for me. If I had someone like your mother, you better believe I wouldn't lose contact with them for anything in the world." She pushed around him, rushed toward her bedroom, and slammed the door behind her. The sound of the key turning in the lock cut through his anger.

What have I done? She didn't deserve the harsh words he'd thrown at her. He took a deep breath and huffed it out. She didn't know what was going on with him, and he didn't want her to know how shaky things might get in the coming days. *Thank goodness I saved enough money to last a few months.* But what would happen after that? Perhaps Carl would let him keep the clients he'd added to the firm for himself. It might be enough.

He heard her muffled sobs through her door. He didn't want

to turn into the kind of husband who mistreated his wife, even if he didn't love her. He did like her, a lot.

He didn't know what to do. Should he let her cry it out? *Probably not.* He couldn't go into her room without an invitation, and he didn't want her to keep hurting from his harsh words.

He paced the length of the house. With his hands clasped behind his back, his steps gradually increased in speed. So many thoughts circled in his mind that he almost felt dizzy.

Finally, he cried out to God. *What am I supposed to do? How can I help my wife? Lord, I don't know how to treat women. I don't want to make a mess of this. Give me some ideas.*

Almost as if spoken out loud, words dropped into his mind. Why hadn't he thought of this sooner?

⁓

*T*raesa tried to smother her crying when she heard Wilson pacing. He continued for a few minutes then stopped. It sounded like he was in the kitchen. Soon he went to the front door and left the house. *Where is he going?*

She wiped her eyes and washed her face in the tepid water on her washstand. She never envisioned anything like this happening in her marriage, especially this soon. Was her life with Wilson going to be like this always? She didn't think she could handle it. But she couldn't leave. She had nowhere to go.

Returning to the mansion was out of the question since they had no idea where Quinton was, and she didn't want to go back to the boardinghouse. She knew they wouldn't turn her away, but she didn't want to face them right now. Her friends there had all been at the wedding. They thought this was a real marriage, complete with love. Would she never feel loved again? Her future spread before her like a vast wasteland—drab, dry, and lonely. How could she face such an existence?

Last weekend had been filled with good things and new friends, and now this. She thought about Carolyn and Henry Stewart and her hopes that they could become good friends. But she couldn't talk to them about what happened. She didn't want to give them a bad impression of her husband. Maybe he'd never treat her like this again. But what if he did?

Lord, show me what to do now. I want to save my marriage.

~

*W*hen Wilson arrived at the parsonage, Henry sat on the front porch in a rocking chair.

"Pastor, can I have a few minutes of your time?"

Henry stood. "I was just enjoying the sunlight after finishing work on my sermon for tomorrow. How can I help you?"

"Could we go someplace private?" Wilson didn't want anyone else to hear about his problem.

"Sure. Come on." He led the way around to the side of the church building, and they entered through the doorway hidden from the street.

The office was small but private. They sat on a sofa along one wall.

"What can I do for you?"

Wilson clasped both hands in his lap until his knuckles whitened. He tried to relax. "I guess I need some marital advice."

The other man chuckled. "We all do at some time or another."

He relaxed against the padded furniture, but it didn't ease his anxiety. "I suppose I should start at the beginning."

The pastor nodded. "That's usually best."

Wilson tried to paint a picture of all that had happened since Quinton reappeared—the man's actions as they affected Traesa, the new wrinkle presented by Carl Johnson and how that could affect his marriage, and the hardest part—how he had treated his wife when he'd returned home from their meeting.

Reverend Stewart bowed his head a moment, then raised it and smiled at him. "I see several problems with what you told me. The main two are your worries about your livelihood and about how you treated your wife. Is that right?"

He nodded.

How was he ever going to conquer that one? "I sure don't know what to do about the way I treated Traesa."

Henry placed his Bible on the small table beside the couch. "Your wife needs to know she's safe with you. That she's the most important person in your life. Evidently you married quickly. Maybe you should court her."

Too wound up to stay seated, Wilson stood to face him. "Now?"

"Yes, now. I'm sure you didn't do much of that before the wedding. How much do you know about her really? What does she like? What are her dreams? Those are the kinds of things a man should know so he can meet his wife's needs."

What do I know about her desires and dreams? Almost nothing.

Henry suggested that he make the effort to learn as much as he could about the woman he'd married. "And always include her in what's going on in your life. She's your partner and help-meet now."

The Bible said something about a wife being a helpmeet, didn't it? Wilson had never thought much about what that meant. Now that he had a wife of his own, he ought to figure it out.

Henry stood to face him. "A wife is God's gift to a man. I've found that most women have a direct connection to God's heart. When my wife makes a suggestion, I always listen to her and seek the Lord about what she says. Most of the time, I find Him in agreement with her. Perhaps you should listen to what your wife said about your family. Contact them and let them know you're married. They will probably want to meet her."

He needed to get home and somehow entice Traesa from her bedroom. He really wanted to know more about her. And he *needed* to apologize to her whether he wanted to or not.

He felt drawn to her in a different way than before their battle of words, and the thought of contacting his parents right now instead of waiting until Christmas brought an ache to his heart. He really did want to see them. The last time he was there, his father had tried to get him to stay in New York City and work with him. Then when he returned to Fort Worth, the law firm became very busy. Maybe he'd been gone long enough for them to accept his choice to move to Texas and practice law instead of going into banking the way his father wanted him to.

"What about your other problem? I know it's hard some-times, but do you trust God? Really trust Him with your daily life?"

The pastor's words felt like a knife slash to his heart. *Do I really trust Him, or have I been trying to run everything myself?*

Silence hung between the two men like a veil, hiding what he didn't want to admit.

He cleared his throat. He was face to face with his greatest failing, not really trusting that God knew what was best for him and Traesa.

"Until this minute, I hadn't realized that I wasn't trusting Him completely." He rubbed the back of his neck. "I'm not even sure I know how to."

Henry opened his Bible. "It's not easy for a man. I've had to go to these two verses many times during my life. Maybe they'll help you. I love how the book of Proverbs talks about real life. In chapter three, verses five and six, it reads, 'Trust in the Lord with all thine heart; and lean not unto thine own understanding. In all thy ways acknowledge him, and he shall direct thy paths.'"

The words became a balm to his hurting heart. Why did he always try to make things work without asking for God's help? When he'd stopped and asked Him earlier today, God had told him to come see this pastor, a man with the wisdom to point him in the right direction.

"Are you saying that God will give me the ability to support my wife if I let Him?"

"Something like that. He has never let me down in that department. Pastors aren't the best paid workers, but Carolyn and I have always had a roof over our heads, enough food to eat, and all the clothing we required. He has also provided everything else that we needed. Sometimes in surprising ways. Maybe He has some surprises you're not letting Him give you and your lovely wife."

Wilson stared out the lone window as the sun moved closer to the horizon, mulling over his words. "I like to take charge of things."

"Doesn't every man?" Henry shrugged. "I've had to learn to choose to let Him have control in my life. And I'm not saying it's easy. But it's the only way I want to live now."

When Wilson headed home in the eventide, his thoughts kept him from seeing what was going on around him. The conversation gave him a lot to think about.

The world looked brighter and his burdens felt lighter.

CHAPTER 17

Traesa didn't want Wilson to know how much his words had hurt her. She hadn't had anyone she loved use words as weapons since she left New York City all those years before. Now her husband had, and he might do it again... and again. She wouldn't be able to stand that. When he'd asked her to marry him, he saved her from the possibility of Quinton attacking her again. The way Wilson talked, she believed he hoped for love to develop between them. Before, she had felt safe with him. Now she wasn't so sure.

The only times in her life when she was loved and protected were with her parents before they died and with her Hilliard grandmother. And both times had come to an end. The Hilliard parents had treated her well, but she felt most loved by Abuela. *Will I ever be good enough for a man to love?* The hole in her heart ached.

What is wrong with me? She stared into the cheval mirror. Sure, her hair was too red and too curly to fit the styles of the day, but even with swollen eyes and tear streaks down her cheeks, she was pleasant to look at. At least, that was what she'd been told by her mother and Abuela.

She had no idea where Wilson had gone or when he would return. *If he returns at all.* Her stomach gave a loud growl that reminded her that she hadn't eaten. She didn't want to wait until Wilson got home. Returning to the kitchen, she resumed chopping the vegetables for the chicken pie she had started before he'd been so cruel. The crust over the vegetables, sauce, and chicken would be light and flaky, just like the cook had taught her. Just the way she loved it.

Her world teetered between a hopeful future with a sense of safety and complete disintegration. Where would she be tomorrow?

~

*W*ilson had been gone too long already, but he took the time to go by the Hilliard mansion before he went home. He told himself that he needed to check on Clara, Alice, and Mrs. Richards. When they finished visiting, he asked the housekeeper if he could pick a bouquet from the flower gardens to take to Treasa. That would be a good way to apologize to his wife.

He held the flowers while he unlocked the front door. After pausing a moment, wondering what he'd find on the other side, he slipped into the parlor. Traesa was nowhere to be seen. *Please don't let her still be crying.* It would break his heart. He had been such a fool. Hopefully, the flowers would help his apology sound as sincere as he meant it to be.

His nose twitched at the amazing aroma emanating from the kitchen. He headed toward the food and heard her voice softly singing a hymn as she worked. He stopped outside the doorway and watched her for a few minutes. She looked so different from the last time he'd seen her. *How could I have lost my temper like that?* The problems in his life weren't caused by her. He almost dropped the flowers and grabbed them quickly.

Traesa whirled toward him, holding a dripping spoon in her hand. "Wilson, I didn't hear you come in."

"I was enjoying your singing." His feet seemed to have a mind of their own as they crossed the room toward her. He didn't want to frighten her again.

She stood her ground, grabbing a tea towel to wipe the drips from the spoon off her apron. But he caught the quick flash of fear in her eyes before she shut it down.

"That smells good." He gave an appreciative sniff then handed her the flowers.

She laid the spoon on a saucer and gathered them into her arms. "These smell wonderful, too." She took a vase he'd never seen before from the cupboard.

There were too many things he didn't know about her as well as what was in their house. How could he make up for that without sounding like a lawyer in court?

He watched her while she put water in the vase and arranged the flowers. The grassy green dress she wore coordinated with the colorful blossoms and enhanced the color of her eyes. She looked beautiful. Why hadn't he noticed that before? Was he too involved in his work and protecting her from Quinton to realize just how pretty she was? God had blessed him with this woman. Now he needed to treat her like the gift she was to him.

Henry knew what he was talking about. Maybe he should heed his other advice.

"Where did you go?" she asked.

Her soft tone touched him more than if she had railed at him. That would be what he deserved for the way he'd treated her.

"I went to visit with Pastor Stewart."

"Whatever for?" Her gaze pierced him as if she were looking for something.

"Needed some advice. He was a big help."

Her brows quirked in puzzlement, but she didn't ask what they'd talked about.

He was thankful because he didn't want to go into all the things he and Henry discussed.

"That doesn't explain the flowers. Where did you get them?" She set the arrangement in the middle of the table and went back to the stove.

He pulled out a chair, turned it around, and straddled it with his arms crossed along the back. "I went by the mansion too. I got to visit a bit with Clara, Alice, and Mrs. Richards."

She frowned. "Why didn't you take me with you? I really want to see my sisters. I'd be able to tell if anything is wrong with them."

He hadn't thought of that. "I'm not sure Quinton isn't watching the house. I didn't want to put you in danger again." He stepped closer to her.

"I try to forget what he did, so I don't think of him often." She opened the oven and used folded kitchen towels to pull a pie pan out.

That was where the wonderful aroma came from, and it didn't smell sweet. "What kind of pie is that?"

After setting it on the hot pads on the table, she turned toward him. "A chicken pie. Christine taught me to make it while I was at the boardinghouse."

"Then it's sure to be delicious." He smiled at her. "Good thing I'm hungry."

She set the table. "We need to let the pie cool a few minutes while I get everything else on the table."

He moved even closer to her and reached for one of her hands. "While we wait, I want to apologize to you."

Her eyes widened.

"I've had a lot of things on my mind, and when I came home, I took my frustration out on you. I shouldn't have. I am so sorry." He gave her fingers a gentle squeeze. "Can you forgive me?"

Once again that flicker of fear sparked in her eyes then quickly died away. How could he make her understand? Take away her fear?

She nodded. "Does Henry know the truth about our marriage?"

The thought hadn't even entered his mind when he talked to the pastor. "I found no reason to share those details with him."

A sigh that sounded like relief slipped from between her rosy lips, and her gaze softened.

"I did tell him about the greeting card incident."

Her fingers stiffened in his hand.

"I made sure he knew I was the one at fault, and he gave me some of his insight into marriage."

Even if he wasn't sure he agreed with everything the man said. Maybe he should take his comments to heart. After all, the idea to visit the pastor had entered his mind soon after he asked God for help.

"Oh?" The question was not only in her one word, but also in her eyes.

"He believes that a wife is a gift from God, and women have a deeper spiritual connection with God than men do. He listens to his wife and considers her opinions."

He held his breath waiting for her response.

After a moment of silence, she spoke. "Did he give you that advice after you told him what you said to me?"

He led her into the parlor to sit on the sofa, pulling her down beside him. Then he leaned forward with his forearms on his thighs. "On the way out to the mansion, I thought a lot about what you said as well as what Henry told me. He thinks I should contact my family and let them know we're married. How would you like that?"

"That will be wonderful!" She leaned closer and squeezed his arm. "And I don't think you'll regret it." A smile as bright as early morning sun shone from her face.

He stood up and helped her up beside him. They headed toward the kitchen and the tantalizing chicken pie that awaited them.

"I'm glad Mrs. Richards let me pick the bouquet from the flowerbeds at the mansion. They look good on the table."

~

*M*onday morning after breakfast, Traesa cleaned off the table. Soon Wilson walked in with a piece of paper and a pencil, pulled out a chair, and sat at the table.

"I want you to help me write the letter to my parents."

She draped a tea towel over the stacked plates. "I'm not sure I'll be any help." She sat in the chair across from him.

He looked as if he were lost in thought. She waited for him to speak.

After staring at the paper for quite a while, he raised his gaze toward her. "I need to apologize to my mother, too, don't I?"

Traesa nodded. His question surprised her. His discussion with Pastor Stewart must have been very interesting. She wondered if he would ever share all of it with her. Memories of her father telling her mother all about his day filled her thoughts. Maybe one day, her husband would do that with her. She could only hope.

He leaned over the paper and started writing. When he finished, he handed it to her. "Read it and let me know if it needs anything else."

She laid the message on the table and slowly read it.

She glanced up at Wilson and caught a smile on his face. "Do you think your family will like me?"

"Of course. What's not to like?"

"When and how are you planning to introduce us?" She handed the paper back to him.

He rubbed the back of his neck. "I'm not sure. If nothing unexpected happens between now and Christmas, we could go visit them."

Her heart leapt within her, almost taking her breath away. "Do you mean it?"

He nodded.

She really wanted to meet his family, but she wasn't sure how she would feel being back in New York City. She probably shouldn't worry about that. His family wouldn't live anywhere near where she and her parents had. And they wouldn't go anywhere near where she spent the time with other orphans. She didn't like to even think about all the things they had to do to get food and clothing. Since his father was a banker, their house would be in a part of the city where she'd never been.

"Do you want to go with me to mail the letter?"

His offer was welcome.

"If you don't think it will be too dangerous for me to go." She reached for her apron strings.

"The way I plan for us to get to the post office isn't anywhere near where Quinton was last seen." He headed toward his bedroom, then stopped and turned back to her. "I need to check with the foreman at the ranch. We could go out there, too, if you want to."

Without thinking, Traesa threw her arms around him and gave him a big hug. She didn't care whether he wanted one or not.

CHAPTER 18

*W*hen they passed the outskirts of southwest Fort Worth, Traesa took a deep breath of the fresh breeze. A few small cottony clouds drifted in the azure sky.

"I love getting out in the country. Nothing to hem us in." She felt Wilson's gaze on her as if it were an actual touch and turned toward him.

His wide smile sparked a twinkle in his eyes. "I've always enjoyed the country too. One of the best parts of my job has been checking on the ranch."

Wildflowers covered the fields all around. "Texas wild-flowers are as pretty as any blossoms found in the gardens of the cattle baron mansions on the bluff above the Trinity River."

"I agree. Do you know the names of any of these plants?" He signaled the horses to turn the wagon onto the long drive that led toward the Hilliard ranch house.

She studied the patches of flowers as they passed by. "The blue ones are Texas bluebells. They and the bluebonnets are my favorites. The orangey ones are Texas lantana. And the pink ones are rock roses. I picked them to make a bouquet for Abuela when I went to the ranch soon after I came to Texas. She always put the flowers in a cup of water, even though they were wilted by the time I gave them to her." That memory brought a smile to her face.

He pointed toward a different patch of flowers. "What about those thin purple ones?"

"Abuela called them vervain. She always loved purple." Traesa closed her eyes, and her mind filled with times when her grandmother dressed in that color. She had so many outfits in various shades of purple. *Oh, how I miss her.* If only she were still with them. Quinton wouldn't have had a reason to show up at the mansion the way he did. She shivered at the memory of his assault.

"Are you cold?" Wilson placed a hand on hers, which were clasped in her lap.

She shook her head. "Not really. I was just thinking about the things that happened after her death."

He gave her hands a gentle squeeze. "Quinton can't get to you now."

Had Wilson read her mind? He sounded so sure, she hoped she could believe his words.

Just before they reached the ranch headquarters, they passed a field with other colors of blossoms.

"Those are prickly pear cacti." Wilson pointed them out.

She liked the way flowers perched on the edge of the large flat sections of the plant. However, she'd learned the first time she came to the ranch that the stickers scattered on the surface were uncomfortable.

"The tall plants in the distance are sunflowers," Wilson said, "but what are those growing between them. I never noticed any like them before."

Traesa gazed toward the patch of blooms. "Those are fireweeds. The petals have the red and yellow colors of flames, and the middle resembles a campfire. My grandmother loved them, too. She told me they weren't for gardens in the city. They belonged in the wild." She couldn't keep the wistful tone from her voice.

Wilson stopped the wagon. "You really miss her, don't you?" His gaze drilled straight into her heart as if he could read her every emotion.

Tears welled up, and she fought to keep them from rushing down her cheeks.

He took her hand. "It's all right to cry. With all that's been happening, you haven't had much time to mourn your loss."

He gathered her in his arms and held her close. She dropped her head to his chest, and the dam holding the tears at bay burst. Soon his shirt was soaked while she muffled her sobs against him. Out there in the open air, her grief flowed freely. She was lost in the pain and anguish of her present situation. If Abuela hadn't passed away, things wouldn't have fallen apart. Somehow, she had to come to grips with the fact that her life had been forever changed.

As her tears and sobs slowed, Wilson patted her back. His gentle touch calmed her. Finally, she slipped away from his warm chest, pulled a hanky from her sleeve, and wiped her eyes and face.

"I must look terrible." She stared across the field toward the ranch house, also surrounded by flowers. "What will Mack and Molly think when they see me?"

With a finger under her chin, Wilson lifted her face until she could see his eyes. "They'll think you're beautiful." After picking up the reins, he started toward the barn in the distance.

Beautiful? He thinks I'm beautiful? Even with tearstained cheeks? She knew that her eyes got red when she cried. Did her husband call her beautiful just to make her feel better? Or did he really think she was?

Soon, they were close enough to see some of the cowboys herding cattle. She'd always been fascinated by the way the cows followed the signals and moved in a mass in the right direction.

Too many people didn't notice signals that could keep them out of trouble. Like Quinton. He'd been a good brother to her before he became friends with young men who led him astray. It was hard for her not to completely hate him for what he'd tried to do to her that last time in the mansion. But deep in her heart, she knew something was very wrong with him right now.

"Are you all right?"

She hadn't realized Wilson leaned so close to her before he whispered the words into her ear.

"I'm eager to see Molly again. It's been quite a while since Abuela and I came to the ranch." She glanced toward the front porch just as Molly emerged from within.

As soon as Wilson stopped the wagon, Traesa jumped down without waiting for him to help her. She hurried toward Molly with her arms open wide. They hugged each other and held tight for quite a while before letting go. Traesa had needed a hug like that for a long time.

Molly pulled away first. "Just look at you. You're so pretty. I guess marriage agrees with you. Aunt Helen sent word that you and Wilson were married. I wish I'd known so I could have attended the wedding. She described it to me in a letter."

Heat filled Traesa's cheeks. "Yes, Mrs. Richards helped me a lot on my wedding day. I like being married."

"Here's hoping I get to experience it sometime soon." Molly's tone tugged at Traesa's heart.

"Is someone calling on you now?" She smiled at her friend.

Molly shook her head. "Not yet, but he might ask Father soon."

"Who?"

"You don't know him. He's a cowboy from a ranch nearby. I don't want to say it out loud because I don't want to keep it from happening."

"I wouldn't know who he was even if you told me his name."

Molly glanced around, then leaned in and lowered her voice.

143

"You never know when someone might be close enough to hear. I'll just have to keep his name to myself for a while longer." She winked and took Traesa's arm and urged her toward the house as Wilson drove the team on to the stables with the wagon. "At least Daddy is out in the stables and wouldn't have been able to hear if I told you his name."

Inside, Molly led her to the kitchen. "Would you like a cup of tea and some cookies? I've made some every day since you got married, hoping the two of you would come for a visit."

⁓

*N*earing the stables, Wilson noticed Mack by the big barn, so he turned the wagon toward him.

Mack looked up when he got close. "Hey, man. Good to see ya. How's married life?"

He had hoped his friend wouldn't ask that question. There were enough lies by omission about his marriage already.

"Hunky-dory." Maybe that would be enough to keep him from asking more questions.

Mack led Wilson through the barn and the stables and to the corral, where most of the horses ran around the fence line. A few of the colts played with each other the way toddlers did.

They ended up in Mack's office where he made his report to Wilson. The herd of cattle had experienced good growth over the first months of the year. Mack planned to take the yearlings from last year to market at the Fort Worth stockyards soon.

When Wilson led the way from the office toward the kitchen, he mulled over all the information he'd acquired that day. Everything looked good to him.

As they arrived in the kitchen, Traesa waited with Molly for them. A platter of cookies rested on the nearby counter. The tantalizing aroma of coffee drew him.

Molly said, "You look as if you would love some cookies and coffee."

"You read me right. That's exactly what I want." He picked up a mug and held it out to her so she could fill it.

"Do you still take your coffee black?"

He nodded. "Yes, I do, especially the wonderful coffee you brew."

~

*T*hree hours later, Traesa stood beside the wagon waiting for Wilson to come back. He and Mack had gone to the spring house for another load to take to Fort Worth. Some things were for Wilson and her, some for the mansion.

"I'm so glad you could come and spend time with me." Molly's smile always lit up the area around her.

"Me, too. Are you and Mack planning to come to town anytime soon?" Traesa was eager to welcome her friends to their new home.

"Probably not for a couple of weeks, since y'all brought supplies for us."

When the men arrived with the last load, the women hugged good-bye. Traesa wondered if she'd ever come back to the ranch. Everything depended on Wilson and Mr. Johnson finding the files that would prove whether she was adopted or not. With that mess of wooden crates stacked in the back room of the law office with no rhyme or reason, she wondered if there was a document to find. She had helped Wilson go through a number of those boxes before Mr. Johnson arrived. She wondered if the man's coming would help or mess up everything. This was surely the reason Wilson had been upset lately.

After he helped her up onto the wagon seat, they headed out. Traesa waved to Molly as long as she could see her waving back.

"Did you enjoy your visit with Molly?" Wilson didn't take his eyes off the road ahead.

She wondered what he was thinking about. At least the expression on his face had changed. Mack must have had good news for him. "I always do. She's a good friend."

They rode along in silence for a while. As they neared the Fort Worth city limits, he turned toward her.

"I'm not going to take you to the mansion, just in case."

"Do you really think Quinton will be nearby?" She clasped her hands in her lap. "Have you had any more reports from the security company?"

"No." He shook his head. "No one has seen him around any of his old haunts. He seems to have disappeared, but we can't take a chance on being wrong. I really need to protect you. I'll take you home. Then I'll take the food to Mrs. Benton. She'll be thrilled with the supplies I brought them."

"Will I be alone at the house?" She really didn't want to be.

"I have a guard watching the house while we're gone. I'll have him stay until I get home."

Traesa whooshed out a relieved breath. How much longer would they have to watch out for Quinton. She had hoped all this would be over quickly. But two months had passed, and nothing had changed.

She thought about the letter they had mailed before heading to the ranch. "Do you think your family will mind that I'm an orphan?"

He pulled over to the side of the street and stopped the horses. "That won't bother them at all. They'll not be able to help but love you."

She welcomed his words. Maybe if his family would love her, he would also. She hoped he wouldn't take too long. Living a lie was a burden in her heart, and she wanted to know that she could trust him completely.

CHAPTER 19

ilson unloaded the vegetables, fruit, and meat they'd brought home from the farm, and Traesa stored them in the icebox. The block of ice had almost melted away, but the ice man would make a delivery early tomorrow.

"I need to talk to Carl before I know when we can go to New York City. I'll stop by to see him on my way home from the mansion."

"I hope you don't take too long. I'll have supper ready by six o'clock."

He headed to the front door. "It shouldn't take that long."

Traesa stood in the doorway and waved at him as he pulled away. He liked to see her doing that. Seemed to build a stronger connection between them. His thoughts turned toward the trip and what it would mean to all of his family. It had been way too many years since he'd seen them. Why had he waited so long to make the choice to contact them again? *Stubbornness, probably.*

Until Reverend Stewart talked to him, he hadn't realized how wrong he'd been by staying away. His marriage to Traesa was a good thing, and he did need to listen to her ideas. This was a really good one. He hadn't realized how his choices had tied him in knots. Now he felt freed from a weight that had accompanied him for so long. He hadn't even realized how heavy it was until it lifted.

When he arrived at the Hilliard mansion, he drove the wagon around to the back of the house. It would be easier to unload the food there.

George Benton stepped out of the gardening shed when Wilson stopped the wagon. "Mr. Pollard, nice to see you again."

"I've brought food from the ranch." He reached for a crate containing wrapped meat.

"My wife will be glad to see that. I'll help you unload. Martha can tell us where she wants us to put everything."

George headed toward the kitchen door. When he emerged again, she accompanied him.

After they reached the wagon, Martha looked at everything. "You brought more than usual, Mr. Pollard."

"Mack said the garden has produced a lot of vegetables, and the peaches are ripe. They have a bumper crop. They had just butchered one of last year's calves. The meat should be plenty tender. Tell us where you want these to go, and we'll soon have them unloaded."

"You can put the meat in the spring house. That spring has surely been a blessing. The water is cold enough to keep the meat fresh for several days. And I'll can some of it to use later."

Wilson enjoyed her enthusiasm. "I wish we had a cold spring at our house. At least, the ice man will deliver every day if we need him to."

Martha picked up a beetroot. "Look at the size of this one. A real giant."

Wilson had to agree with her.

"The root vegetables will go into the cellar and the other vegetables and fruit in the icebox." She headed into the kitchen with her arms loaded.

Before he left, Wilson talked to Mrs. Richards to see if she needed more money. She told him the girls were safe and happy, enjoying their summer break from school. Just what he needed to hear.

The sun was lowering toward the western horizon when he reached the law office. The lights were on inside, so he headed toward the door.

Carl sat at his desk and looked up when Wilson entered. "Was everything all right out at the ranch?"

"Just fine." Wilson dropped into a chair across from Carl. "I want to talk to you about something that has happened." How much should he tell the man? Not everything about his own family, for sure.

Carl sat back in his chair. "So what's going on?"

Wilson decided to start with the office. "I'm not sure this law firm can support two families very long. Your uncle and I were both single men, and we did fine."

"So how many active clients do we have right now?" Carl reached into his drawer and retrieved a pad and pencil.

Wilson went to his own desk. He picked up the list he kept and handed it to Carl. "The people with a check by their names have left the firm for other lawyers."

After perusing the list, Carl handed it back. "That's quite a few. How much business do they represent?"

"Some of them only needed occasional help, but others kept us pretty busy. Like the Hilliard estate. I had planned to ask you if I could keep that account, since I'm so familiar with their needs." He laid the list back on his desk.

Carl stared out the window as if he were considering everything Wilson told him. "I thought the Hilliard account would be yours. My uncle had investments and savings I inherited, in addition to the law firm. Let's keep things the way they are for a while and see what happens. We can change it anytime we need to."

That was better than he'd expected. Perhaps they could

acquire more clients. A lot of people were moving to Fort Worth recently. "That sounds good to me."

"Anything else on your mind?" Carl hadn't gone back to his files.

Good. "I wrote to my family in New York City, letting them know about my marriage."

Carl's eyes widened and a questioning gaze quirked his eyebrows. "That's interesting."

"I want to take Traesa to New York City to meet them."

Carl glanced at the wall calendar behind their desks. "When would you like to go?"

"I hope my father can send the private railcar in Fort Worth for us to use. We'll have to wait to hear back, but I hope it will be sometime in July."

Carl leaned forward again. "I didn't realize you came from wealth."

"My father owns a bank. He really wanted me to go into the family business, but I wanted to be a lawyer. Your uncle was one of his childhood friends. Dad contacted him, and I came out here to learn the law." For a moment, memories from those early years flashed through his thoughts. He really missed Mr. Harrison, who'd been almost like a surrogate father to him.

"How long did you work with my uncle?"

"Eight years. And I've taken care of the Hilliard account for five of those years."

"Since you took over that account even before my uncle died, I would consider the Hilliards to be your clients." Carl jotted something on the pad. "So how long do you plan to be gone?"

Wilson had no idea. He and Traesa hadn't had time to discuss all the details. "I'm not sure. It'll take us over a week to go both ways. I don't know how long we'll stay. We'll probably be home in two or three weeks." He sure hoped his estimate was right.

"I can handle the firm for that long. The trip would probably be good for you and your wife." Carl's smile supported his statements.

Wilson glanced toward the window. The sun had almost reached the horizon. He would have to hurry, and he still might not make it home before six o'clock. It was too early in their marriage to disappoint his bride.

~

*T*oday had been such a special time with her husband. The letter they'd mailed told his family that they wanted to visit them in New York City.

Traesa sat at the kitchen table to plan supper. At the boardinghouse, Christine taught her to make a country fried steak that was so tender, it almost melted in her mouth. With this fresh beef, she'd pick out the best pieces for their supper. Because of the cream gravy for the steak, she'd make mashed potatoes. The gravy would be good with the potatoes too. She'd also prepare carrots glazed with honey. And those peaches would make a delicious cobbler. She had eaten one soon after they arrived at home, and the juice had dripped down her chin. There were plenty peaches for the cobbler and some for them to eat fresh.

She gathered all the ingredients for the dessert, and soon it was in the oven. Some of the cream she'd bought the day before was left in the icebox. It would be delicious poured over the cobbler.

Traesa barely finished cooking by dinnertime. Wilson should be home any minute. She wanted the table to look pretty, so she picked a few flowers and set the vase as a centerpiece.

She had kept her ears tuned to what was going on in the street outside. Once someone came by riding a horse. Wilson had hired the wagon from the livery stable, so he'd be riding home. She hurried to the door to meet him, but a stranger rode by.

Disappointed, she stepped back from the screen door and paced. She had their food on a warming shelf on the wood-burning stove. If Wilson didn't get home soon, nothing would taste as good as it would right now.

Finally, she dropped onto the couch to rest. Because she was tired from their day and cooking supper, she fell asleep. The squeak of the screen door opening woke her. When she opened her eyes, Wilson stood just inside the doorway looking at her. She sat up straight.

He walked toward her. "I'm so sorry I'm late. All the conversations took longer than I thought they would. Will you forgive me?"

The pleading in his tone touched her heart. How could she not?

She stood. "I just hope our supper is still edible."

"I do too. I'm hungry, and something smells good."

They walked into the kitchen together.

"Sit down." She turned to the stove. "I'll fix our plates."

He didn't sit, instead watching her every move. "This all looks delicious."

The food would have been better an hour before, but she didn't mention that. Sometimes, she couldn't understand her husband. Actually, most of the time.

When she put the filled plates on the table at each place she set, he joined her as she sat down.

She got up immediately. "I steeped some tea and chipped ice to cool it." Opening the icebox, she removed the tall glasses and brought them to the table.

Wilson took a long draught. "This tastes so good. My mouth and throat were dry. I'll say grace."

With their heads bowed, he thanked God for the food, for

the hands that prepared it, and for the wonderful time they had today.

After he took a bite of his steak, he slowly chewed. "This is delicious." He grabbed another bite. "You haven't made this before. I love it."

She tasted hers, and it was much better than she'd thought it would be after sitting so long. "I also made a peach cobbler. Save room for dessert."

He had just put a forkful of potatoes and gravy in his mouth, so he didn't reply right away. "That sounds wonderful."

After the meal was over, he helped her put the leftovers in the icebox, and they washed and dried the dishes together.

"I talked to Carl about the trip, and he agreed we could be gone for two or three weeks."

They were really going. She'd get to meet the rest of her family. Tears filled her eyes, but she was able to keep them from running down her cheeks.

This was going to be an adventure...she hoped.

CHAPTER 20

J<small>ULY</small>

*T*oday was the day. Traesa and Wilson would board the train in the family's private railcar. She couldn't even imagine what it would be like. The car had arrived two days earlier, but Wilson hadn't wanted to take her to see it then. He said she would see it later today and that would be soon enough.

She packed a small trunk with the latest fashionable clothing Abuela had made for her before her death. A carpetbag contained the essentials she would use on the trip. The trunk would be in the private car with them if she needed anything else during the journey.

Wilson had taken her out to the mansion last night. They parked the buggy behind the house where no one on the street would see her alight from the conveyance. She had enjoyed the time spent with her sisters while Wilson met with Mrs. Richards and the rest of the staff.

Clara and Alice had hugged her so tight, she almost felt like one of the family again. And they were full of questions about where she had gone and what she was doing. She answered the best she could without giving them much information. They were thrilled that she and Wilson were married.

After she and Wilson arrived back home, they went to bed. Excitement kept her from being able to sleep well. Evidently, Wilson didn't have the same problem. Each time she got up and walked around in the house, she didn't hear a sound from his bedroom, not even a snore. Surely, she'd be able to sleep some on the train.

After the hearty breakfast they'd shared that morning, Traesa hadn't had anything else to eat. Her stomach felt a little queasy, probably from the excitement. Wilson told her when he went to work for half a day that he would grab something to eat before he came back to the house.

She wandered out on the front porch and enjoyed the pretty flowers in their garden and the yards of most of the houses on the street. Glancing all around, she tried to spy the guards Wilson said were out there somewhere. Then she walked around the house looking for them. Those security guards could really hide themselves. Wilson told her there would be two guards around the clock all the time they were gone. If only they could find Quinton, none of this would be necessary.

When she arrived back at the front porch, a rather large coach turned onto their street. It stopped outside their house. Wilson opened the door and climbed out, and the driver stayed on his seat, holding the reins.

"We'll go to the train station in this. It will keep us mostly hidden and can hold all our luggage." He stepped to her side and offered her his arm. "Are you ready?"

She nodded. Chills ran up and down her spine.

"Are you sure you packed everything you need?" His eyes sparkled with excitement, too.

"I hope so." She preceded him into the parlor.

He took her hand in his. "I want you to enjoy our trip. The

train will stop in some towns before we arrive. If you need anything you didn't pack, we can buy it for you."

She liked the way he had been treating her since their first quarrel, almost as if he were courting her the way William courted her sister Charlotte before they married. Maybe he was. If so, it made her happy. Maybe their marriage would become real…sometime.

"And don't worry about my family." He gave her fingers a gentle squeeze. "You will fit right in."

"I hope so. Since I've lost all of my family, yours is mine now." She gave him a shy smile.

"Of course they are." He put his arm around her shoulders. "Now show me what I need to load into the coach."

She felt anticipation growing during the whole ride to the Texas and Pacific Railroad Station south of downtown. People in buggies were parked in marked spaces north of the building. Their driver went right past the line and around to the other side. A long train waited on one of the tracks.

Wilson helped her down from the coach. "This train is very different from the one you came on. It has the latest 50-ton engine, so there's less smoke and soot. And it can pull more railcars." His gaze traveled up the length of the waiting conveyance. "I see passenger cars, freight cars, and a few I can't tell what they are. At least one is a dining car, maybe more with all these passenger cars."

"There was no dining car on the orphan train." She lifted one hand to shield her eyes from the hot summer sun. "And the engine looks new."

"Where did you eat?"

She really didn't like to remember much about that train ride. "The adult who rode with us brought baskets of food that lasted a few days. When the trains stopped to take on water, they got off the train and bought more food."

Her glance slid all the way down the train to where they

stood beside the caboose. The one right in front of the caboose caught her attention. It was different from anything she'd ever seen. Looked almost new too. Painted a shiny dark green, it had larger windows than the other passenger cars.

"That's the private car we'll be riding in." Wilson must have read her thoughts. "We'll be comfortable there."

The coach driver climbed down and helped Wilson transfer the luggage.

Wilson led her up the steps into the railcar, though this didn't feel like a railcar. Comfortable chairs scattered throughout the space, some attached to small tables with lamps on them. Luxurious carpet and draperies enhanced the room, and the windows were clear and bright.

"How soon will we be leaving?"

Wilson smiled at her. "In about fifteen minutes. The other passengers are in their seats already."

The butterflies in her stomach swarmed again. She placed her hand on her abdomen as if to stop them. Everything in her life was changing again, hopefully for the better.

Two chairs, with a table and lamp between them, were angled toward each other. What a wonderful place to have a conversation with a friend...or husband. She settled in one of them and arranged her skirt to get comfortable.

Wilson turned from the window he'd been staring out of, almost as if she had called him to her, and took a seat in the other chair. "I just saw the engineer head out of the depot. We should start moving soon."

That would be great. "He has to start the engine. That takes a while, doesn't it?"

He laughed. "It sure does, but the engine is idling. It doesn't produce much smoke or steam until we start moving."

A knock sounded on the door.

"I'll see who that is." He got up and hurried to the door.

A man stood on the other side. Traesa had never seen him before. He was tall with a maroon suit.

Her husband welcomed him in. "This is Martin Jones, Traesa. He works for my father. He'll take care of us on the journey. Martin, this is my wife, Traesa."

The man smiled, taking off his hat and holding it with both hands in front of him. "I'm glad to see Mr. Wilson got married. The family is so eager to meet you."

Traesa chuckled. "I am too. Eager to meet them and glad Wilson married me."

The men joined her laughter.

"Did Mr. Wilson show you around this place?"

"Not yet. We just came aboard." Her husband answered the question before she could.

"This is the main area. Most of your time will be spent here." He headed toward the back of the railcar. "There are sleeping compartments on both sides. On the front end of the car, my compartment is on one side, and the lavatory area is on the other." He pointed to each thing as he mentioned it. "A table is attached to the wall right there, and I'll raise it up before I go to the dining car for your food."

"Of course, you can go to the dining car if you prefer." His dark copper skin tone glowed when he smiled at them.

The man placed his cap back on his curly black hair. It matched his suit exactly, a shade of burgundy that was close to the uniforms the conductors wore. She would have thought he worked for the railroad if she hadn't been given the correct information from her husband.

The wheels began to turn, causing a kind of clackety-clack when they connected with the rail.

Mr. Jones gave a slight bow. "I'll go to the dining car to see what is going to be available for dinner."

Traesa thought supper was coming up.

~

$\mathcal{W}$ilson watched an expression of confusion pucker his wife's brows. When Martin exited, he turned to her. "What's the matter?"

She gazed at him. "Are we going to have two more meals today?"

His hearty laugh filled the room. She loved it when he did that. His laughter brought joy to everyone around.

"He's from New York City. They have breakfast, lunch, and dinner, while we in Texas have dinner and supper."

That brought up a faint memory from before her parents died. They did use those names for the meals. She'd been in Texas so long she hadn't thought about it for years.

He slid back into the chair near hers. "This should be a better trip than the one that brought you to Fort Worth."

"It already is. We rode in a stuffy car with windows that were stained with smoke and soot. We couldn't see much through them. We were in a private car, but it wasn't anything like this one."

He leaned forward with his forearms on his thighs. "I'm so sorry you had to go through that, but we wouldn't have met if you hadn't come to Fort Worth. I'm glad God brought you to the Hilliard family. I know He still has special plans for your life."

"I hope so." She wondered what they could possibly be.

As the train picked up speed, the bumping smoothed out a lot.

"Our train rattled along the tracks," she said, remembering. "If we opened the windows, it was only a little at the top. Smoke and soot came through every crevice." She shuddered.

He put his hands over hers clasped in her lap. "Now they have a new kind of filtering system that keeps most of that from coming inside the train."

She sighed. "Thank goodness." She took a deep breath. "It's so much better than I remember."

By the time they were out of the Fort Worth metropolitan area and well on their way, Martin returned. "The galleys have lots of fresh food since this is early in the trip. Would you like to go to the dining car, or should I bring your food here?"

Wilson turned toward Traesa. "Which would you prefer?"

She studied his face before she answered. "Today, I'd prefer to eat here, if that's all right with you."

Martin took a small writing pad out of his pocket. "They have steak or chicken, mashed potatoes and gravy, pickled beets, and a salad."

"Do you prefer steak or chicken?" Wilson asked.

"I'd love a steak. I didn't eat much today. I was too excited. And the vegetables sound wonderful."

He glanced back toward Martin. "Two steaks."

"They also have either peach cobbler or apple pie for dessert."

"Peach cobbler—"

"Apple pie—"

Both she and her husband spoke at once.

Martin pulled a pencil from his pocket. "Two steak dinners and both desserts. I'll have this back here in two shakes of a lamb's tail."

As he exited, he and Traesa both laughed.

When she stopped laughing, she asked, "Where did that come from?"

"Martin's father herded the sheep on one of the farms just outside the city. That was often said in their family. He first shared the phrase with me when we were in school together."

"Interesting." Traesa smiled at him. "I like learning more things about you."

Wilson wasn't sure what he'd expected the trip to be like. He loved every minute of it. When they were between towns, he and Traesa talked more than they ever had. About things they liked and stories of happenings before they met. When the train had a longer stop, they left their car and walked around the area close to the depots.

At the longest stops, he took her shopping. Her smile always brought one to his face. She wanted to take a gift for each person in his family. He helped her pick those out. She also added to her own belongings. Sometimes, she chose things she wanted, and sometimes he found a gift he wanted to give her.

One time, when they returned to the train, he asked her to tell him the best gifts she'd ever been given and learned that, except for Christmas, the only gifts she'd received since her parents died were the ones from her grandmother. This information made him want to give her more presents for no reason. Maybe this is what Henry meant when he talked about Wilson courting Traesa. Her reactions to the things he bought her pleased him.

He was thrilled to show her his favorite places along the way. Maybe next time they came on this trip, they could take more time so she could see even more of this wonderful country where they lived.

If there is a next time.

CHAPTER 21

NEW YORK CITY

When they disembarked, Traesa glanced all around. She'd boarded the train at the Grand Central Depot with the other orphans, but she'd been dazed, overwhelmed. Back then, Grand Central had been at the very edge of the city. The depot was the same, but in the eight years since she'd left New York City, the area around the train station had changed—more buildings, more people, more modes of transportation filled the area.

"Come." Wilson took her hand and led her past the caboose to the other side of the tracks. Martin followed them to where a wagon and an open carriage were parked.

A man stepped out of one of them and approached. "Mr. Wilson, it's so good to see you."

"I'm glad to be home again, Gerald." Wilson shook his hand then slid his arm around her waist. "This is my wife, Traesa."

"I'm glad to meet you, ma'am." He tipped his hat then looked back at Wilson. "I brought the surrey, sir, because it'll be a much cooler ride with the open sides."

She glanced at the vehicle. The wind fluttered through the red fringe around the top, while the rest of the surrey shone in the hazy sunshine. Someone took good care of it. Perhaps Gerald did.

"Walter will help Martin load the luggage into the wagon and drive back to the house. We'll go ahead of them." He climbed into the driver's seat while Wilson helped her up into the back of the surrey and joined her. He put his arm around her shoulders. "Are you comfortable enough?" he whispered in her ear.

All she could do was nod. She wasn't used to him holding her like this, but she liked the feeling. As if he were trying to protect her. As if their marriage were normal.

Soon after they left the depot, Gerald turned away from where Traesa used to live. He followed one street for several blocks then turned into an area of neighborhoods with charming cottages, most with white picket fences and small flower gardens in front. As they continued, the houses became much larger with plenty of yard space for lovely gardens. Traesa enjoyed the colorful displays that emitted enticing aromas into the warm summer breeze. Some of the houses even had fancy fences surrounding them.

They turned onto a driveway leading to a set of large ornate, metal gates. The red bricks of the driveway matched those on the house. A man stood beside the gates and opened them to let the surrey drive through. Her husband waved, and the man nodded back at him. She peeked over her shoulder and watched the servant close the gates behind them.

Wilson helped her down with his strong hands on her waist. "Welcome to my family's home, Traesa." His warm breath caused a shiver to skitter down her spine.

"It's beautiful." Her words came out as a whisper because his touch made her breathless.

The front door burst open, and a beautiful older woman hurried toward them. "Wilson, welcome home."

Traesa saw where her husband got his good looks. His mother's hair was dark brown with a hint of a wave like his. She had the same hazel eyes as her son.

He spread his arms wide in time to catch her in a hug.

She laid her hands on his cheeks. "My precious son, I've missed you so much."

He dropped a kiss on her forehead. "I've missed you too. I'm sorry I took so long coming home." He pulled her against him, then stepped away and turned toward Traesa. "Mother, I want you to meet my wife, Traesa. She's the one who made me realize I needed to make this trip to visit the family."

His mother took Traesa's hands and gave her a bright smile. "Traesa, thank you so much and welcome to the family."

Those words were music to her ears. She truly had a new family. "Your welcome warms my heart, Mrs. Pollard."

"Please, call me Evelyn." Her mother-in-law opened her arms, and Traesa walked into the best hug she'd had since Abuela died. Tears of joy gathered in her eyes. When they parted, she pulled a handkerchief from her sleeve and patted her cheeks dry.

The two women went up the wide front steps while the men unloaded the luggage.

A butler had the double doors open for them. Evelyn escorted her into the parlor, and they sat on the wingback tapestry sofa. A silver tray took pride of place on the marble-topped coffee table.

Evelyn picked up the flowered china teapot and filled two matching cups. "What do you take in your tea, lemon or milk?"

The refreshing smell of the hot beverage made Theresa realize how thirsty she was. "I like both sugar and milk."

"So do I. How many spoonfuls of sugar?"

"Two." She watched her mother-in-law scoop the sweetener

with a polished seashell shaped silver spoon with a filigree handle. It looked so dainty.

Then Evelyn handed her the teacup and saucer. "It's good to have you and my son here. I hope you'll stay a while."

"I think we'll be here about two weeks."

A bright smile lit up Evelyn's lovely features. "Good. We'll have time to get to know you, and you might enjoy doing some shopping."

Wilson entered soon enough to hear his mother mentioning shopping. "Of course, she will. Doesn't every woman?"

Evelyn rose and hugged her son again. "Would you like to have tea with us? Mrs. Hardy made cookies and finger sandwiches for our tea."

Wilson frowned. "Finger sandwiches? Really?"

"Oh, Wilson. They aren't made of fingers." She picked up the plate. "They are just small sandwiches. They're all the rage for teas and parties these days. These are cucumber." She pointed out each kind as she named them. "Here are egg sandwiches, ham, and smoked salmon with cream cheese. Try them. They're delicious."

"Pour me some tea." He took the plate and offered it to Traesa first. Then he picked up one and put the whole thing in his mouth. A smile lit his face. "I know why they're so popular. This is delicious."

Traesa chose two, but each one was too large to put in *her* mouth all at once. Evelyn handed her an extra saucer for her sandwiches.

Wilson sat in the matching wingback chair before his mother handed him his tea.

"Are they already here?" A girl's voice came from the hallway, accompanied by the sound of feet scurrying down stairs.

The voice sounded somewhat familiar to Traesa. How could that be? She hadn't known anyone who lived on this side of the city.

Wilson set down his tea and rose in time to catch a beautiful young woman in his arms.

"Oh, Wilson, I'm so glad you're finally home again." She reached up and planted a kiss on his cheek.

Traesa felt a twinge of what had to be jealousy. She had never felt anything like it before. This man was her husband, and another woman shouldn't be hugging him so tightly or kissing him. She would have to put a stop to that if she could figure out how to do it. How long were they going to continue hugging?

She glanced at her mother-in-law and found her smiling at the two. Was this one of his former girlfriends? She had no idea how many he might have. They hadn't discussed that on the train ride. Her heart dropped like a stone to her stomach, and she was beginning to feel sick. The bite of sandwich she'd just taken turning sour in her throat.

He pulled the woman tighter and swung her around before letting her feet drop to the floor.

Evelyn stood. "Gwendolyn, what are you doing here? I thought you and your family would be here for dinner tonight."

The young woman dropped her arms from Wilson and turned toward Evelyn. "I couldn't wait to see my brother again."

Her brother? Now Traesa could see the resemblance. She let out her breath. Something else besides the sound of his sister's voice felt familiar. Maybe just because she favored her brother. She had the same hazel eyes, but she must have gotten her honey-colored hair from their father.

Wilson moved beside his sister. "Sis, this is my wife—"

"Traesa Kildare!" Gwendolyn stared at her. "How are you? I've thought of you so many times after I returned home from that orphan train."

Gwendolyn had been one of the women who'd accompanied the group of orphans she'd been in.

Tears prickled Traesa's eyes. "I remember you. You were kind to me when no one else was."

Wilson walked to Traesa and pulled her to his side. "This is amazing. I'm glad you were there for my wife when she needed someone the most."

Now tears glistened in Gwendolyn's eyes. "Me, too."

"On our train ride, she shared more about the trip. How there were so many stops and no one chose her." He held her even closer.

"That's amazing." Evelyn stood up from the sofa. "After she returned home, Gwendolyn talked to me about you. And now you're a member of our family." She gestured to the table, sofa, and chairs. "Let's sit and finish our tea time."

After they were seated, her mother-in-law poured tea for her daughter and passed the plates of sandwiches and cookies around the group.

Gwendolyn leaned forward. "I'd have recognized you anywhere. You've lost most of your freckles, and your bright red hair has darkened some, but I could never forget your green eyes. I looked into them so many times on that trip. I want to know how you and my brother met."

"Let's wait until tonight when all the family is together," Evelyn suggested.

∼

*W*ilson and his brother-in-law Victor met with his father in the study before dinner. His father sat in his favorite leather chair smoking a cigar. He laid it on the edge of the ashtray on the table beside his chair. "I want you to know how sorry I am that I insisted so much that you work for the bank. I'm proud of you. Before he passed away, Harrison let me know what a good lawyer you were."

He never thought he'd ever hear those words coming from

his father's lips again. Something inside him clicked. "Thank you for telling me. I do enjoy my work, and my clients need my expertise."

"Victor is a really good banker. If you had stayed, Gwendolyn might never have met him, and Evelyn and I wouldn't be enjoying the grandchildren they've given us."

A blush crept into Victor's cheeks, but his chest expanded as if with pride. Maybe he wasn't used to talking about that aspect of marriage. It's a good thing the man and his sister had children. His parents might not ever get any from his and Traesa's marriage. Of course, if he and his wife ever fell in love, they would.

"I've been enjoying the electric lights in the house. When did you add that to the mansion?" He tapped the lamp on the table beside his chair.

"You've been inside since you arrived. If you'd gotten here after dark, you would have seen that the whole neighborhood has electric lights now. Didn't you notice the poles?"

"Not really." He had been talking to his wife and watching her reactions.

Of course, the Hilliard mansion and others in Fort Worth had electricity, even the boardinghouses. But there were lots of areas that didn't, including their cottage. The first neighborhoods they entered after they left Grand Central Depot didn't either.

From the doorway, Mom said, "Benjamin, dinner will soon be ready to be served. We should all get dressed for it."

Dad smashed the end of the cigar against the ashtray until it stopped smoking then stood. "We must join the women. I'm sure Mrs. Hardy made all your favorites, Wilson, and I'm glad. Our tastes are very much alike."

CHAPTER 22

*I*n the Pollard mansion, Traesa enjoyed all the space filled with beautiful furniture, paintings, decorative vases, and exquisite porcelain figurines. The place was similar to the Hilliard mansion, and couldn't be more different from the humble home where she and Wilson lived.

She tried not to make comparisons with their little cottage in Fort Worth and the two mansions, but she couldn't help it. Although she loved the home she shared with Wilson, maybe someday, they could afford something a little larger. They would need something bigger if they had children. She wondered if that would ever happen.

Wilson led her upstairs to where they would be staying during the visit. "Here we are. It's one of the guest suites."

The room was bright and lovely. The wainscoting, window frames, and door frames were painted a pale, creamy color, and the wallpaper had the same color background. Dark green vertical stripes with flowers in various shades of pink and blue scattered over them rose above the wainscoting to the high ceiling.

"It's beautiful." She sighed. "Even the quilt on the bed has the same colors worked into it."

He pulled back the soft green lace curtains and fastened them open. Then he faced her. "Traesa, we can fix up our bedrooms if you'd like. They wouldn't be as fancy as this, but we could make them prettier."

His words went straight to her heart. He'd noticed something she liked and wanted to give it to her. That boded well for their growing relationship, didn't it?

She looked once more at the bed. Wilson didn't want his family to know theirs wasn't a real marriage, so they'd put them in the same room. *What am I going to do?*

He opened the door to the left of the bed. "This is the bathing room with a water closet on this side."

She followed him into the area. A claw-foot bathtub sat under the window. Since they were on the second floor and there weren't any close neighbors, she'd be glad to use the tub. She peeked inside the open door of the water closet.

"It's wonderful to have these so close to our bedroom." *Why did I say "our bedroom?"*

"We won't need to sleep in the same bed." He smiled at her, evidently reading her thoughts again.

He opened another door. "This is the dressing room. There's a chaise longue in here. I can sleep on that."

But that would be too small for him to stretch out and sleep comfortably. "I'll sleep in here. You can have the bed."

A frown crossed his face, and he stepped closer to her. "I want you in the bed. I would never ask you to sleep in the dressing room." He reached toward her then dropped his hand.

She almost wished he would hug her like he did his mother and sister. Maybe someday soon he would.

"We could compromise. Take turns with the sleeping arrangements." She gave him her brightest smile.

"You have a lot of good ideas. This one is not one of them. I insist on my idea." His smile took the sting out of his words.

She glanced around the spacious area. A large wardrobe sat against one wall. It had double doors with mirrors and four drawers below. She opened one door and found that the maid had hung up her dresses. When she opened a drawer, her unmentionables were there. She quickly shoved it closed and glanced over her shoulder, a blush creeping up her neck. She stood and turned around. A room-sized rug woven in a Persian design with the same colors used in the bedroom padded the floor. If he chose to sleep on the floor, maybe he would be comfortable.

He opened the cedar chest at the foot of the bed. "I'll get what I need from here before we go to bed, so I'll be all right."

Traesa knelt beside the chest and went through the items stored there. Sheets, pillowcases, quilts, and blankets. He should be able to sleep well with some of these.

Wilson headed toward the door.

She stood. "What should I wear for dinner?"

Her words stopped him, and he turned toward her. "Traesa, you always look pretty in whatever you wear."

Although his words made her feel good, she still didn't know how they dress for dinner.

"Since this is a special occasion for celebrating," he added, "I'm sure most of the family will dress up, but it's not formal."

That's a good thing since I don't have anything formal to wear.

"Something you'd wear to church would be fine." He took her hand and led her toward the dressing room. His warm clasp sent flutters to her stomach like a flock of hummingbirds.

When he reached the wardrobe, he opened the door she had opened before. After letting go of her hand he pulled out a green dress she wore to church. It was one of her favorites. Lace that flowed down the front of the skirt like a waterfall and decorated her sleeves was dyed to match the fabric. Mother of pearl buttons fastened the bodice from her neck to her waist.

He laid it across the bed. "I've always liked you in this dress. It accentuates your lovely eyes."

His gaze met hers, and she couldn't look away. A strong connection sizzled between them. He took a step toward her then stopped. With a slight shake of his head, he left the room, shutting the door behind him.

She clasped the dress close to her chest. He'd called her beautiful a couple of times recently, and now he had complimented her again. Did that mean he was beginning to have some deep feelings for her? Was it a first step toward making their marriage real? These thoughts thrilled her...and scared her. Was she ready for more than they had together right now?

Soon after Wilson left, Gwendolyn arrived, and a young woman followed her into the bedroom. "Maria will help you get ready. I hope you don't mind."

Traesa had donned her dress. "Of course not. Wilson told me tonight was a celebration, but not formal, and I was trying to decide how to wear my hair."

"Then it's a good thing I brought her," Gwendolyn said. "She's wonderful at dressing hair."

When Maria finished and Traesa looked in the mirror, she was amazed at the woman she saw. For the first time, she felt as beautiful as her mother and Abuela said she was. What would Wilson think?

~

Wilson was sitting in the parlor where he could see the staircase. The maid descended in front of his sister, so he arose and stepped into the foyer.

Traesa stood on the top step. She smiled when she saw him.

The most beautiful woman he'd ever seen came toward him.

When he'd visited her grandmother, she'd often stayed in the room with them while they visited, only leaving when they discussed business. He'd seen her dressed for church, but her beauty had remained partially hidden from him. Tonight, he recognized how amazingly beautiful she really was. What was he going to do about it? They had an agreement, and he planned to adhere to it.

He closed his eyes and took a deep breath before opening them. He approached his wife and offered her his arm so he could escort her in to dinner.

In the dining room, they were seated side by side. They could talk to each other and to the people on the other side of each of them, but he wouldn't have to look at her all night. She would have been a distraction. They really needed to be careful about how they would answer the questions he knew were coming.

When everyone was seated, his father said the blessing for the meal. Immediately, the servants started setting the food on the table.

"Wilson, how did you and Traesa meet?" His father asked a question he'd expected from his mother or sister.

He glanced at his wife. She gave a slight nod.

"I was her grandmother's lawyer for the last four years. She passed away a few months ago."

"So you've known each other for four years. That's good."

His mother glanced from Traesa to him. "Did you see her every time you went to see her grandmother?"

"Most of the time Traesa was with her grandmother."

The servants had finished bringing the food, and he gazed over the bounty.

"Mrs. Hardy did indeed fix my favorites. I'll have to thank her later."

Traesa took a slice of ham and passed it to him. The next dish by him was scalloped potatoes, then green peas, followed by a garden salad. He wondered what the dessert would be. He hoped it would be a chocolate meringue pie.

"I take it that you married after her death." His father wouldn't leave the subject alone.

"Yes." He took a deep breath. *Tell the truth, but only what is asked.* "There was some trouble with her brother, so I helped her. After a while, we married."

"I wish we could have been at the wedding." His mother's bottom lip trembled.

When everything was happening in Fort Worth, how his decisions would impact his mother hadn't even entered his mind. He regretted that more than he could express. His selfishness that didn't want to hear any more discussions about him becoming a banker from his father had hurt his mother. He wished there was a way to make it right, but he couldn't think of a way. Why had he let this happen? There was no good reason.

"I'm so sorry. I made a mistake when I didn't keep in touch with you better."

"Let's let bygones be bygones." His mother gave him a tremulous smile. "At least, you've brought your lovely wife to meet us."

"Our pastor told me I should listen to my wife because wives have a direct line to God."

His father laughed. "I'm sure he's right. Your mother has been very helpful to me with her spiritual discernment."

His mother smiled at his father. "Thank you, Benjamin. You've always been my mainstay."

"As I should be. Marriages are like that. I pray that yours and Traesa's marriage will be as strong and long-lasting as ours is."

After the meal, they went into the parlor and visited for hours. He loved watching his wife interact with his family. He would need to bring her back at least a couple of times a year.

The last thing his mother said to them was, "Remember,

Traesa, we'll go shopping tomorrow, and Wilson can spend time with his father and brother-in-law."

His wife was smiling as they climbed the stairs to go to bed.

$\sim$

*T*raesa had enjoyed the evening immensely. Her family had grown a lot today. What a wonderful feeling. Gwendolyn and Mason hadn't brought their children tonight, but she would get to meet them tomorrow before the women went shopping. Two nieces and one nephew. She hoped that someday she and Wilson would give them cousins.

Her husband opened the door to their bedroom and held it for her to enter. "What do you think about my family?"

"I loved them, and I'm glad they are my family too." She sat on the side of the bed. "I'm so glad you listened to Reverend Stewart's suggestions or this never would have happened."

Wilson stood in front of her, his gaze roving over her face. "I owe you an apology for not listening to you in the first place. One of my biggest regrets is that day when I yelled at you. I know this is a marriage of convenience right now, but you are my wife, and I should have respected you more than I did."

"We all make mistakes. Of course, I forgive you." She stood. "Gwendolyn helped me put this necklace on. Could you take it off?" She turned her back to him and leaned her head forward so he could see the clasp.

Abuela had given her the gold necklace with three emeralds that rested at the base of her neck for her eighteenth birthday. She hadn't worn them many times, and there had always been a maid to help her take it off. His warm fingers on the back of her neck sent gooseflesh all over her body.

When he finished, he handed the jewelry to her, then went to the cedar chest. After choosing what he wanted to use, he turned back to her.

"Goodnight, Traesa. I hope you sleep well." Then he went into the dressing room.

She knew she would sleep well, and after the time with the family, she would have sweet dreams too. She whispered a prayer of thanks before she started to dress for bed.

~

*W*ilson wished he'd listened to Traesa about the sleeping arrangements. The chaise longue was not comfortable. He had twisted and turned, trying to get positioned where he would drop off to sleep. After he did, his feet hung off the bed. He awoke in the middle of the night, and his feet had gone to sleep. He stood up, and almost fell down. He sat down and rubbed his feet to get the feeling back into them.

After pulling all the bedding off the chaise longue, he made a bed on the floor. With thick carpet on the floor, he was finally comfortable, and he slept until morning. He got up and dressed, then folded up all the things he used. He picked the bedding up and opened the door, intending to put it all back in the cedar chest.

Traesa stood beside the bed facing him. She was yawning and stretching, which pulled her nightgown close to her body. The sunlight from the window behind her revealed the shape of her body through the thin cotton.

He gulped, and his mouth went dry. His heartbeat accelerated, and his body awakened. He quickly looked away. He was a man, and he reacted to his wife, but that wasn't love. It was lust. His wife deserved more than that. He moved to shut the door, but Traesa must have heard the movements.

Her arms quickly dropped, and she clasped them in front of her bosom. "Wilson, I didn't know you were up."

"I haven't been up long. Just enough time to dress and fold these." He glanced down at the bedding. "I was ready to return them to the cedar chest, but I can wait." He turned to go back to where he came from.

"No need to. I can go in the dressing room and prepare for the day."

She walked past him. She smelled as good after a night's sleep as she did during the daytime, like roses and something else he couldn't define, but he liked it.

∼

*T*wo weeks flew by like a whirlwind, with Traesa meeting so many people the names scrambled together in her head. And getting acquainted with the real New York City was an adventure, especially visiting the Statue of Liberty with Gwendolyn. Since Mother Pollard had a committee meeting, she and her sister-in-law went alone.

As they stood on the wharf on the harbor, Traesa stared up at the historical statue.

"It's pretty amazing, isn't it?" Gwendolyn's words interrupted Traesa's thoughts.

She nodded. "I had no idea how massive it would look from the shore."

"Do you want to climb up and look out from her crown?"

Do I? Traesa couldn't imagine doing such a thing. We could walk around the island and look at the statue up close."

While they boarded the ferry to the island with about twenty other people, Traesa kept glancing at the colossal monument. Something about the statue tugged at her heart. When they arrived at the wharf and they deboarded, she and Gwendolyn walked all around the base of Lady Liberty and looked at her from all sides.

Back where they started, Gwendolyn once more asked her if she wanted to climb to the top.

She craned her neck to look at the torch in the statue's hand. "I've never been that high before. I'm not sure what I'd feel like."

"You'll never know if you don't try. Everyone has come out smiling."

Finally, she relented. Inside the structure had lots and lots of steel supports. In the very center, a spiral staircase went all the way to the top.

Gwendolyn walked to the foot of the structure and held onto the banister. "Look how sturdy it is." She mounted the first step, then turned toward Traesa, holding out her hand. "Come on."

Traesa stared at her as she walked up a few more steps. With her heart pounding, she followed.

By that time, Gwendolyn was several steps even higher. There was no way Traesa could climb that fast. She clung tight to the banister as they ascended, watching her new sister-in-law move farther and farther away. As they climbed, they met occasional people coming down the other side of the staircase. Most of them greeted her, but she kept her gaze fastened on Gwendolyn.

Finally, a little over halfway, she looked down and froze. Then she glanced around. The walls seemed to be closing around her.

Terror rose up inside her. She had a hard time catching her breath. Her hands began to sweat, and her heart felt as if it would pound right out of her chest. She couldn't take another step...up or down.

What was she going to do? She couldn't let go of the banister. She was trembling so hard she was afraid she would fall all the way to the bottom.

She had never fainted in her life, but that was a distinct possibility. Her mouth and throat were so dry, she couldn't make a sound.

She closed her eyes tight, so she wouldn't see what was

around her. She dropped to sit on the step above the one where she stood, but she still clung to the banister.

She sat there with a ringing in her ears that blocked out everything going on around her.

"Traesa!" Gwendolyn's voice coming from beside her finally penetrated the sphere of fear that held her in its grip. "Traesa, I'm here. What's wrong?"

Gwendolyn's arm around her loosened some of her fear.

She opened her eyes. "I...I don't...know."

"Did something happen?"

Traesa took a breath...then another. "I've never felt like this before."

Gwendolyn peeled Traesa's fingers from around the banister, one by one, and pulled her even closer.

A woman, who had ridden the ferry at the same time they had, climbed toward them with worry wrinkling her brow. "Is she all right."

"I'm not sure." Gwendolyn still held her tight.

The woman knelt on the step right below them and gave Traesa a sympathetic smile. "I think I might know."

"Tell us please." Gwendolyn's voice had a pleading tone.

"My daughter has claustrophobia with a fear of heights." Her gaze focused on Traesa. "Some people have that. Some people don't. It's not something you can control."

"So...how will I...get down from here?" Traesa's words came out on a whisper.

The woman stepped up to be level with them. She helped Traesa to rise. "We will put you between us and hold you from both sides as we go down. Or we can walk one in front of you and one behind you, if you prefer."

*W*ilson paced from one end of the upper hallway to the other. *Where are my sister and my wife?* They had been gone much longer than they said they would be. Maybe he should have gone with them instead of spending time at the bank with his father and brother-in-law.

The two women should have called to let him know they would be this late. Didn't they know he would be worried about his wife. The women had done a lot of things in the last two weeks, but they returned on time.

As the door burst open, he reached the top of the stairs after the third time he'd been back and forth. Gwendolyn entered with her arm supporting Traesa.

Anger rose up within him, and he didn't even try to tamp it down. His wife's face was almost as white as snow, and half of her hair had come loose from the elaborate style she had when they left.

He rushed down the steps. "Where have you been? What happened to my wife? Who did this to her?"

The two women stopped and stared at him. Gwendolyn apparently insulted, and fear flickered in Traesa's eyes.

"Calm down, brother. No one did anything to your wife. She—"

"Then why does she look like that?" He reached them and held his arms open to Traesa.

She moved from beside Gwendolyn and dropped her face against his chest. He gathered her up in his arms and turned toward the stairs.

He glanced back at his sister. "We'll talk about this later."

When he had Traesa in their bedroom, he took a deep breath and relaxed. "Would you like to lie down?"

She shook her bed. "I can stand up."

When she was on her feet, she didn't pull out of his arms.

"Please don't be angry with Gwendolyn. I found out something about myself today."

He leaned his head close to the top of hers. "What was that?"

"That I have claustrophobia and a fear of heights."

He enjoyed having her in his arms. That could mean there was hope for their marriage...someday. "Just how did you find that out."

After her complete explanation, she added, "Because of all this, we missed the return ferry and had to wait for the next one. So did the lady who helped me and her husband."

"At least, you and Gwendolyn didn't have to wait alone." He kissed the top of her head. "I'm so sorry."

"Why are you sorry."

"First, for getting angry before I knew what happened. Second, because I should have gone with the two of you instead of going to the bank. I was supposed to keep you safe."

She finally stepped out of his arms. "It wasn't your fault. No one knew that would happen, but I do think you should go apologize to your sister."

"Of course." He headed out the door.

CHAPTER 23

August

*T*raesa stepped up into the private railcar. This time, she felt like she belonged there. After all, she was a Pollard. Wilson had placed a long-distance call from New York to Carl Johnson at the law office and received his approval for them to extend their stay one extra week. That allowed her to become even more involved with them. What a blessing to now have that extended family.

She sat in one of the comfortable chairs and pulled a book out of her pocket. She could read until her husband arrived. While they were in New York City, she hadn't even picked up a book. There had been so much to do.

Not able to concentrate on the story, she closed the book and placed it on the table beside her chair. Then she revisited the memories of their adventures.

Wilson entered the car followed by Martin. Immediately, she felt the train begin to slowly move and build up speed.

He slid into the chair on the other side of the lamp table. "Well, Mrs. Pollard, did you enjoy the visit?"

She loved it when he called her Mrs. Pollard. "Of course, didn't you?"

A smile spread across his face. "Immensely. What was your favorite part?"

How could she answer that? Everything was wonderful! The time with family. Getting to know their nephew and twin nieces. Maybe someday she and Wilson would have children as cute as they were. Shopping. The opera. Sightseeing. Meeting his church friends. Too many things to name.

"The best thing was finding out that Gwendolyn is your sister, and now she is mine. The next best thing was the wedding reception your family had for us at the Waldorf Hotel last night. I never expected anything like that."

He smiled. "That was rather nice."

"Did you know everyone would bring us presents?"

"That's normal for New York City. I'm just glad I could find a trunk that would hold the gifts and all the things you bought."

A smile crept across her face. "What are we going to do with all of them when we get home?"

He leaned forward with his forearms on his thighs. "We can keep them in the trunk until we get a larger place."

"I hope that happens sooner rather than later."

Martin came out of his sleeping quarters. "What would you like for lunch today? Should I go check on what they're having in the dining car?"

Wilson leaned back in his chair. "That's a good idea. Did my mother give you the ingredients and recipe for that Waldorf salad we had at the hotel?"

Martin nodded. "She did. I'll prepare it here in the railcar to go along with whatever else you'll be eating."

Wilson stood and held out his hand to her. "Let's go out on the observation platform while he prepares our meal."

The train didn't get up to full speed until they would leave the outskirts of town, but they still felt the wind generated by the movement of the train. Martin must have noticed her holding her curls away from her face, because he had them stand near the back wall of the railcar, so they were protected from most of the wind.

"You told me that you stayed with your grandmother when most of the family attended events."

She stared up into his smiling face. "Yes."

"Then how did you learn to dance so well? I enjoyed every dance we shared at the reception."

"When the dance master came to teach the other girls to dance, I participated in the classes, too."

Wilson stared out at the passing scenery. "So you weren't really just a companion for Mrs. Hilliard."

"No. She didn't call me that, and neither did I. Actually, no one in the family did until the words poured like venom from Quinton's mouth." Those words accompanied by his actions felt like knives thrust into her heart. She shut the door on those thoughts. She would not let her erstwhile brother destroy the joy she experienced on this trip.

"We have got to find the proof we need." His expression as he looked down at her fed the hope in her heart.

Traesa enjoyed the trip, and she wondered how she would feel to be back home in Fort Worth. Had the security guards found Quinton? She couldn't decide if that would be a good thing or not.

$\approx$

*T*wo days later, Wilson watched the train pull into the station in Fort Worth. *Home at last.* On the side of the train away from the depot was an open coach and a wagon, each with a driver. Carl had everything waiting for them. With Martin's help, they had the luggage loaded into the wagon in a short time.

"Thank you for the help." He gripped the servant's hand and shook it. "How soon will the private car be going back?"

"They think there will be a train to connect to by tomorrow. I'll stay with the railcar until then."

When Wilson brought Traesa off the train, Martin tipped his hat toward her.

"Thank you for taking such good care of us." She smiled at him.

"You're welcome, Mrs. Pollard. I hope we see both of you again real soon."

"Me, too." She took Wilson's arm while they went to the waiting conveyance.

The loaded wagon followed the coach as they made their way toward their house. Wilson kept watch all around them the best he could. He didn't see anyone who reminded him of Quinton.

At home, after dispatching the driver who'd unloaded their trunks, Wilson went into the house and found Traesa busy unpacking. "How can I help?"

She smiled up at him. "I'm so glad to be home. I'm enjoying putting everything where I want it to go. Do you need to see about other things since we returned?"

"Actually, I do. Several." He headed toward the kitchen door then turned back. "Don't worry about getting supper together. We can eat at the boardinghouse this evening."

"That would be nice." She nodded and turned back to the luggage.

He went out to the small barn behind the house. He'd had the security guard feed and water his horse. Since Golden Girl hadn't been ridden while they were gone, she was eager to get outside. He currycombed her before he put on the saddle and bridle. He added saddlebags in case he might need them.

After he mounted her, he had to keep a tight rein so she

wouldn't gallop. Maybe before he got home he could take her for a bit of a run.

First, he headed to the Smith Security office, hoping Jed would be there. When he walked in, a couple of the security guards who had worked for him before were sitting in the outer office.

"Is your boss in?"

" He knew you were coming home today. Go on in."

Wilson hadn't told him. "How did he know that?"

"Carl Johnson let him know. Jed figured you'd want to check in with him."

He knocked on the paneled oak door.

"Come in." Jed looked up as he stepped into the room. "Wilson, good to have you back. How was your trip?" He stood and shook Wilson's outstretched hand.

"My wife and I enjoyed it." He did especially, because he learned so much more about her on the train trips.

"Must have since you stayed an extra week."

"You don't miss much, do you?"

"That's my job, knowing what's going on. Especially with a client. Have a seat." He gestured to one of the two chairs in the room. "I assume you want a report."

Wilson nodded. "I saw that the house is fine. What about Quinton?"

Jed leaned his elbows on his desk and steepled his fingertips. "I'm not sure whether you need us anymore. We've been combing every inch of Fort Worth and the surrounding areas and interviewed lots of people who know him. No one has seen him since that day he stopped by the boardinghouse back door for a handout."

"That's interesting."

Jed settled back into his chair. "We even interviewed the kitchen help at the boardinghouse. They said he'd been around a lot until that day, but he hasn't been back since then."

"I'm surprised he hadn't seen Traesa before that time."

"I believe Hilliard is either dead or has left this area. Do you want us to keep searching and guarding your house, or should we stop?"

Wilson pondered that question for a moment. "How about we stop the search, and you just continue to post guards at our house and at the Hilliard mansion?"

"Sounds good to me." Jed looked like he was thinking about something serious. "There was one other thing. A body was found near the Trinity, but not very close to where Quinton was last seen. He was beaten so badly that no one could tell what he really looked like. He did look like a bum with long hair and beard, as Quinton was the last time he was seen. And his clothes dirty, smelly, and ragged as well."

"Did anyone claim his body?"

"No." Jed stood. "He was buried in a pauper's grave."

Wilson wished they could know for sure whether this man was Quinton or not. Then those worries would be gone.

"Send last month's bill to the law office. I'll take care of it right away." Wilson stood and shook Jed's hand again. "It's good doing business with you."

His next stop was at the law office. When he went in, Carl wasn't at his usual desk. Wilson went through to the file room and found him going through yet another crate.

Carl stood up when he entered. "So the wanderers are home at last."

"And it's good to be here." Wilson dropped on a short stack of crates. "I'm guessing you haven't yet found the documents we need."

"You'd be right about that."

"How's business going?"

"Actually, rather well. A couple of the clients who went to other lawyers have come back to us. They liked our service better. Let's go into the front office."

They did, and Carl picked up a paper from his desk and handed it to Wilson.

He perused it and saw the names of the returning clients. "I'm surprised. These two were the most vocal about not liking what I was doing before they left. Maybe my marriage made a difference."

"Might be." Carl sat in his desk chair.

"How are things with the Hilliard account?"

"I think everything went smoothly," Carl said. "I kept the records for you to go over. It's about time to take more money to Mrs. Richards. I have the envelope ready." He pulled it out of his drawer.

"That was going to be my next stop."

"Then it's a good thing I went to the bank today. Tell Mrs. Richards hello for me. I enjoyed getting to know her while you were gone."

Wilson took the envelope and put it in the inside pocket of his suit coat. "I'll see you tomorrow."

He enjoyed the ride to the mansion just as much as his horse did. There were areas where there were no houses, so he let her run.

When he arrived, Henry O'Neal met him at the stable and took charge of Golden Girl. Wilson found the housekeeper in her office.

She glanced up from what she was working on when he walked in the door. "Mr. Pollard, welcome home. I'm so glad to have you back." She got up and stood before him. "Did Traesa have a good time on the trip?"

"Indeed, she did. My family absolutely loved her. It turned out that my older sister was one of the women escorting the orphans on the train."

"It's a small world, isn't it?"

"Yes. I've not seen her so happy since her grandmother died. She fit right in. She'll want to know how Clara and Alice are doing."

"They're having a wonderful summer. Would you like to see them?"

"Not right now, but I'll pass that along." He reached into his pocket and withdrew the fat envelope. "I brought you more household money."

"Thank you." She locked it in a drawer in her desk.

"I'm going to take Traesa to the boardinghouse for supper. She'll be tired after she finishes unpacking. We brought back a lot more than we took with us."

Tears glistened on her eyelashes. "I wish I could be the one having supper for you here."

"Maybe you can soon. The security firm has had men searching all of Tarrant County for Quinton, and they haven't found even a trace."

~

*O*hen Traesa and Wilson walked into the boardinghouse, Mary Kelley greeted them. "I heard you went on a trip."

Traesa smiled as they hugged. "Yes, I got to know Wilson's family. It was wonderful."

"Before you go, Bridgett, Christine, and Sheila will want to see you. Molly will enjoy waiting on you."

As soon as they were seated by the windows, Molly hurried toward them. "Traesa, you look so lovely. I'm happy for you, but we really miss you here." She looked at Wilson. "Thank you for taking such good care of our friend."

Her words warmed Traesa's heart. She loved having a larger family, but the women who worked here were almost like sisters to her. She felt truly blessed.

After they ordered, their conversation was interrupted first by Bridgett. Then Christine and Sheila came together to welcome them back.

After everyone left their table, Wilson took Traesa's hand in his. "I'm glad we went to see my family...I mean, our family, but you have so many people who love you here, too."

"I finally realize they are like relatives to me."

"And don't forget those at the Hilliard mansion *could* very well still be your family. I hope we soon find out something about what's going on with the legal process." He gave her hand a slight squeeze before letting go to place his napkin in his lap.

"So has Carl still been searching the files?"

"Yes, in between taking care of the clients. A couple of them who left the firm have come back. That's good for both Carl and us."

Molly set their food in front of them, and Wilson took her hand again while he said a blessing over the food. She enjoyed his touch. He had been doing that more lately. Taking her hand and touching her shoulder or her back when he walked with her. Just thinking about it brought a warm shiver up her spine.

"I also went to see Jed Smith at the security company. His men have been unable to find anything about Quinton. Maybe soon, you can go back out to the mansion. Mrs. Richards wants to have us there for a meal."

Traesa's heart leapt. That would mean she could spend more time with Clara and Alice. Her deepest desire was for them to truly be her sisters once again.

CHAPTER 24

*W*ilson and Traesa settled into their regular schedules without incident. Today was a beautiful day. The oppressive heat of August had broken, and the temperature was a little cooler in comparison. He whistled his favorite hymn as he rode to the office.

As usual, Carl had already arrived, even though Wilson was a few minutes early. No matter how early he came to work, Carl was already there. Maybe the man didn't have anything else to do but work since his wife was still in Iowa.

"Good morning," Carl said.

"A very good morning to you too." Wilson picked up the mail on his desk. He rifled through the envelopes to see if he needed to take care of anything right away.

"You're in a happy mood. Did you have a special weekend?"

Wilson dropped the envelopes on his desk and turned toward Carl. "Nothing out of the ordinary. Traesa and I always go to church on Sunday, and the pastor's message spoke straight to my heart. Of course, it often does. Then the pastor and his wife invited us to have dinner with them."

Carl cleared his throat. "And what church do you go to?"

He perched on the back corner of his desk. "New Hope. It's near where Traesa and I live. Not a big church, but it's growing all the time."

"Sounds like a church I might like to attend."

"I know they'd be glad to have you. They welcomed Traesa and me with open arms the first Sunday we went. Pastor Henry counseled me earlier in our marriage. Made it better."

"Tell me the address and service time. I'll try to come next week."

Wilson got out a pad and pencil and wrote the information on it. "I sometimes forget details. This will help you remember."

He handed the paper to Carl.

"I have good news, too."

"I like hearing that." Wilson slipped into his desk chair.

Carl picked up a file, and there was another under it. "These are two new clients. They both came in when you were out checking on some of your clients yesterday."

"That's wonderful. So I guess you didn't have much time to work in the file room."

Carl laughed. "Not for the last few days. But we've been making good headway with our search. We're three-fourths of the way through."

"And we still haven't found a single document that will help me with the Hilliard estate. That's disappointing."

"At least, we'll be able to find all the files when we finish."

As Carl went back to the files he had been working on, Wilson attacked the stack on his desk, both files and mail.

Carl cleared his throat. "I know you've been having the security company search for Quinton Hilliard. Have they found him yet?"

How should he answer this question? He hadn't told Carl all about the relationship with Quinton.

"Not yet. They've searched Tarrant County and can't find a trace. I'm inclined to think he's either dead, or he has left this area. He could be anywhere." That's what bothered him a lot. What if they never found him? They couldn't search the whole country.

"Remember when Hubert was looking for me, I was in Alaska. He didn't find me until I came back to Iowa. Hilliard could be in Canada or Alaska, even."

"Or he could be back East, but I don't think so. Maybe California, or down South, or somewhere in the Rocky Mountains. There's nothing we can do about it now."

About a half hour before time for the noon meal, the front door opened, and a stranger came in.

He took off his hat and held it at his side. "Which of you men is Wilson Pollard?"

Wilson walked around his desk. "How can I help you?"

"Who is he?" The stranger nodded toward Carl.

"He's Carl Johnson, the senior partner in this law firm."

"I'm Theodore Collins from Waco." The man held out his hand, and Wilson shook it.

Theodore turned to Carl and shook his hand too. "I was going to ask Mr. Pollard for a private meeting, but what I have to ask him could affect you."

Wilson gestured toward the chair on the other side of his desk then slid back into his own chair. "How can I be of service to you?"

"It's kind of a long story, but I'll try to be brief." Theodore leaned forward as if eager to tell the tale. "My uncle and aunt raised my twin sister and me after our parents died. I am now a junior partner in his law firm. Our aunt has been ill for quite some time, and the doctor finally recommended that she go to Mineral Wells to see if the Crazy Water can help her. Of course, we all wanted her to go, so they left this morning. We have a very important case that needs a lawyer with more knowledge than I have."

A sad story, to be sure, but Wilson wondered what this could have to do with him.

"My uncle was good friends with Mr. Harrison. He knew about you, Mr. Pollard. How you ran the firm after the man died. He had followed some of your cases and respects you as a lawyer. He would like for our firm to hire you to come to Waco to help me with the case."

He lifted a hand out. "I don't think I'd be interested in that."

"Please hear me out. We would only need you a week or two. You could stay in our large home with my sister and me, or we could put you up at a hotel. We really need the help." He leaned back in his chair and huffed out a breath.

Wilson glanced at Carl, and he nodded. "A week or two wouldn't be a long time. I can take care of things. I've been thinking about having Lillian come here to see if she likes Fort Worth. This would be a good time to do that."

Why hadn't the man brought Lillian here before now? It would be a good idea if he planned to stay with the firm.

"Mr. Collins, I'd have to talk to my wife before I can give you an answer. How long will you be here in Fort Worth?"

"As long as it takes." The man must be desperate for his help.

"I'm going home for lunch in a few minutes. I'll talk to her about it. If you can return around two, I should have an answer for you."

⁓

Traesa heard the front door open just as she pulled the main dish from the oven. Wilson's footsteps hurried toward her.

He stopped in the kitchen doorway. "That smells so good. Is it what I think it is?"

"And just what do you think it is, Mr. Pollard?" She couldn't keep a teasing tone out of her voice.

"Why chicken pie, of course, Mrs. Pollard."

She set it on a trivet in the middle of the table. "I know it is one of your favorites."

"And so are you, Traesa." He picked her up and swung her around in his arms.

She couldn't keep from laughing with him. He'd never done that before. It was just like he did with his sister. Maybe he thought of her like a sister, since she wasn't a real wife...yet. Hopefully, someday...

Back on her feet, she turned toward the cupboard and pulled two plates from a shelf, trying to hide the blush she felt fill her cheeks. She'd planned to have the table set before he got home but hadn't gotten it done.

"Why did you leave work early?"

He pulled his usual chair out from the table and sat in it while she finished putting everything on the table. "Don't you want me to be here now?"

"Of course, I do. I was just surprised." She sat in her chair and started serving up the food.

"When we finish eating, I have something to talk to you about." He took his first bite of the pie. A smile bloomed on his face as he enjoyed it.

She loved making him happy. When she had talked to Carolyn Stewart one time, she said that one of the ways she exhibited her love to her husband was making his favorite foods. Was that what she was doing? Letting him know that she loved him? Because she did. After all the time they had been together, she knew he was an honorable man. Loyal. Honest. Above reproach. Everything she'd ever dreamed about in a husband. If only...

"This is delicious. You're such a good cook. Every day I look forward to the meals you prepare."

And I love it when you compliment me. She wished she dared to speak the words aloud, but she couldn't unless he said them first. *I love you.*

After they'd finished eating a slice of the apple pie she'd made earlier that morning, Wilson stood. "Let's go sit in the parlor so I can tell you what happened at the office."

He followed her with his hand touching her back as if he were guiding her where to go.

The story he revealed amazed her. She would have never expected something like that. Not in a million years.

"What did you tell Mr. Collins?"

"I needed to talk it over with my wife."

That surprised her almost as much as the proposal the man from Waco made to her husband. Before they had gone to New York City to visit his...their family, he made all the decisions without asking her anything about it. Having him want her opinion made her feel special.

"Would you want to go to Waco for a week or two while I helped Theodore with his important case? We would stay in a nice hotel there." His words had an almost pleading tone.

A two-week adventure sounded nice.

"I'd like that. When would we go?" She'd have to do quite a bit of packing.

"As soon as we can get there. How long would it take you to be ready?"

"I can start packing this afternoon. We should be able to go tomorrow. What time does the train to Waco leave the station?"

After he told her, she nodded. "We can make that one."

∾

*W*ilson returned to the office while whistling a happy tune. He arrived almost an hour before he expected Theodore.

Carl looked up as Wilson entered. "So what did your wife think about the offer?"

"She agreed."

"It must be nice to have such an accommodating wife. I hope Lillian will be agreeable to coming here. I've been gone from home quite a while."

"Perhaps she'll jump at the chance to come." *How could she not?* Wilson wouldn't want to be away from Traesa that long, and they weren't in love with each other. Maybe someday...

CHAPTER 25

*T*raesa watched out the train window as they approached the city. "I didn't realize how large Waco is."

Wilson smiled at her. "Have you been here before?"

"No, but I thought it was a small town."

"A lot is going on here on the Brazos River. Several colleges, lots of churches, even a Jewish synagogue. One nickname is Jerusalem on the Brazos."

She had never heard any of that.

"Once the suspension bridge across the river was built, ranchers could drive cattle across it to take them to market. Waco grew a lot after that. You'll find a lot of interesting things while we're here."

The train slowed as it approached the depot. The sounds of iron against iron and the clackety-clack of the wheels on the tracks created a loud cacophony. The hooting whistle announced its approach. Steam and smoke drifted around the engine as it came to a full stop. No wonder people were drawn to the dramatic event of the arrival of the train.

A crowd milled around outside. People meeting those who

disembarked and others waiting to take their places in the passenger cars.

Traesa wondered if the lawyer who'd asked Wilson to come to help him with a case was somewhere in the crowd.

Her husband led her down the aisle then descended the steps to the platform. He turned back and offered his hand to help her off the train. His thoughtfulness made her feel special, as if she were completely his wife. She hoped this attention would continue.

A young man with blond hair was making his way toward them. A young blond woman followed.

Wilson caught sight of him and held out his hand. "Theodore, it's good to see you again."

Mr. Collins shook it, then addressed the woman beside him. "This is my sister, Dorthea." He turned to her. "This is the man I've been telling you about."

"I'm glad to meet you, Dorthea." Wilson gestured to his wife. "This is Traesa."

The woman appeared to be around her age. Perhaps they could become friends.

The Collins twins had a coach nearby. While the men loaded the trunk, the women started getting acquainted.

"We have a suite for you at the McClelland House Hotel." Dorthea spoke with a soft voice. "I assume you and I will spend a lot of time together because the men will be working long days on the case."

"That sounds wonderful."

~

*A*fter Wilson helped Traesa get settled in their rooms, he left promising to return before supper time.

Theodore waited in front of the hotel with an open carriage. "You can use this for the duration of your time here.

We also have horses at our place, in case you want one to ride."

"Thanks. The carriage will be great for when both Traesa and I go anywhere, and I'd love to have a horse to ride when I'm alone." He climbed in the conveyance.

Theodore headed toward downtown, where his office was located. He parked the carriage behind the building and took the horse into the small, barn nearby. Wilson followed him. Two of the four stalls held horses.

Theodore put the carriage horse in another one. "I'll send my secretary to rub the horse down while we visit about the case."

By the time the men finished their meeting, it was five o'clock. Both of them stretched.

Theodore frowned. "I forgot to ask you something my sister wanted to know."

"What's that?" *Is his sister involved in the law practice, too?*

"She wanted me to ask if you and your wife would come for supper tonight. I was supposed to send word if you can't come. It's too late for that."

Wilson didn't usually accept invitations without talking them over with Traesa, especially since he'd been trying to do what Henry suggested. Maybe she'd be all right with his decision.

"Sounds wonderful. I'll have to go back to the hotel and tell Traesa, and I need to clean up." He started toward the door then turned back. "What time should we be there?"

"We usually eat at seven. You can take the carriage back to the hotel. I'll send my coach to pick y'all up. He'll be there about six-thirty. Will that give you enough time to get ready?"

Wilson smiled as he thought about how long it might take his wife. "Enough for me, but I'm not sure about Traesa."

Theodore went to the telephone hanging on the wall. "I'll

call the hotel and have a message sent to your room. That will give her extra time."

I hope it's enough.

~

*W*aco was a wonderful town to visit. Traesa dressed in her coolest dress and most comfortable shoes. Today, Dorthea was taking her downtown to visit some of her favorite places. Since they were so close in age, they enjoyed many of the same things.

Dorthea arrived in an open carriage, and she was early enough that a gentle breeze kept them cool. "I'll show you as many things as I can today, then you and that handsome husband of yours can come to our house again for supper. Our cook always enjoys cooking for visitors."

"That will be nice." *And Wilson and I won't need to find a place to eat.* Both she and her husband enjoyed spending casual time with the Collins siblings.

By the time the two women arrived back at the hotel, Traesa was exhausted, but it had been an exciting day. Wilson hadn't come home from the office yet, so she soaked in the bathtub in the bathing room in their suite. She had just finished dressing when he entered.

"Traesa, I'm home." She laughed, but he was right. This was their home for however long they were in Waco.

She met him in the parlor. "Did you have a good day?"

He stared at her with an expression she couldn't read. She'd never seen it before.

"We got a lot done. How did you spend your day?"

"Dorthea took me to some of her favorite places. There's an Old Corner Drug Store where they sell sodas. They're cold and delicious. There's one the pharmacist Charles Alderton created in 1885. It's a mix of 23 flavors. The drink was originally called the Waco, but then it became Dr. Pepper. I think I want to go there every day to get one."

His eyes twinkled. "Maybe we can go together one of the days. I'd like to try it. I'll have to hurry to get cleaned up so we can get to the Collins home in time for supper.

~

*W*ilson hurried home to be with Traesa. Today, he and Theodore had finished a little early. He was enjoying his time with his wife more and more. She was having a good time with Dorthea, and he was missing all the fun. Maybe when the men were finished with the legal case, Traesa could show him all the places the women had visited.

He opened the suite door and entered. Before he could say anything, she was standing in front of him.

"So what did you and Dorthea do today?"

"Did you know that cotton is a major crop in the area around Waco?"

"No, but I'm not surprised." He couldn't hold back a smile. Her joy was contagious.

"We saw where the cotton is ginned. There were many tufts of white on the ground around the gin. And long lines of wagons waited their turn."

He headed toward his bed chamber. "I'm going to wash up before we go to supper."

When he came out clean and in fresh clothes, Traesa sat on a chair reading the paper. "So did you go anywhere else while you were out?"

She smiled. "Back to the Old Corner Drug Store for more of that Dr. Pepper. Then Dorthea drove through some neighborhoods where various historical houses were. She told me the stories of who built some of them. Then we went by Baylor University, which moved here from Independence, Texas, to

Waco in 1886. It's an amazing school of higher learning. And there's Paul Quinn College for Negro students."

He was glad Traesa had a new friend and was enjoying Waco.

~

*T*hen the day came when his wife asked the question he hoped she wouldn't.

"Have you seen the information about the Crash at Crush?"

"Yes, I have, and I think it's a mistake." He knew she'd want to go see it.

"It would be interesting to see what will happen."

Her smile told him how much she wanted to go. How could he prevent her from attending?

"Mr. Crush doesn't have a lick of sense if he thinks that will be safe." There he'd told her what he thought about the whole-staged-train wreck thing.

She frowned. "According to what I read, Mr. Crush is convinced it's all right. Evidently, he talked to the engineers who built the steam engines, and they've assured him nothing will blow up."

He paced around the parlor in their suite. "Have you ever been close to one of those engines?"

"I've ridden several trains. Why would the railroad do what he says if it's dangerous? Some railroad staged a train wreck somewhere back East. A lot of people went to see that, and no one was hurt."

"I'm telling you that will be not only dangerous, but some people might get killed." Exasperated, he wanted to shake some sense into her, but that wouldn't help their relationship. "Besides, the crash is supposed to take place fourteen miles from Waco, near the West stop on the rail line. That's too far for you to go."

"Dorthea will go with me. Or maybe you can take some time off and accompany me." Her voice contained a beguiling tone, but it didn't touch him.

"I'm not going. Neither are you. Period."

Her pout didn't bother him. He was adamant about wanting to keep her safe. He'd protected her from Quinton, and now he had to keep her safe from herself. It. Wasn't. Happening. No matter what.

When he was at the office with Theodore the next day, he brought up their conversation.

"I'm afraid my sister may have been a bad influence on your wife. She has a mind of her own. I haven't ever been able to stop her from doing something she's determined to do."

Wilson hoped Traesa would listen to him instead of Dorthea.

CHAPTER 26

*T*raesa answered the knock on the door of their hotel room wondering who it could be. Wilson wouldn't be knocking. "Dorthea, come in. Should I order tea and finger sandwiches for us?"

"I didn't come just for a visit."

Traesa could believe that. She had never seen her friend dressed so casually. "Come in and have a seat. I'm glad to see you anytime. So why did you come by?"

Dorthea leaned forward eagerly. "I'm going to Crush, and I plan to convince you to join me."

"I shared what Wilson said with you the last time we were together. He told me not to go. Remember?"

"I know he did. He and my brother don't think women can think for themselves. We are both adults, and we can make our own decisions." Dorthea leaned back in her chair. "You know that the Suffrage Movement is making great strides. Wyoming granted the right to vote to women in 1869, and several other states have since then. That proves women have good sense."

"I knew about that."

Dorthea smiled. "Can you truthfully tell me that you don't want to go?"

Could she? No. She shook her head.

"Our men have been working late almost every day. We could get there, watch the wreck, and be home before they get home. We don't even need to get close to the wreck. We could stay back partway up the hill surrounding three sides of the valley."

Traesa didn't want to go against Wilson's wishes, but this was a once in a lifetime chance. She really, really wanted to go.

~

*T*raesa watched Dorthea as she drove the carriage along the road heading east from town. The roof of their conveyance shaded them from the early afternoon sunlight, and the open sides allowed a breeze to cool them.

"This suspension bridge is a marvel, isn't it?" She glanced down at the Brazos River flowing south under them, wondering how deep the water was.

They reached the other end of the bridge, and the road curved north. As they continued, Traesa enjoyed the wooded hillsides and occasional farm and ranch houses they could see from the road. Some places had cattle and horses in the pastures.

Other fields boasted cotton bursting open. People with long white sacks hanging from their shoulders bent to pluck the bolls as they walked between the rows.

Dorthea slowed the horse. "I'm glad I don't have to pick cotton. It's back-breaking work."

"I can see that." Her back almost hurt just looking at the pickers.

Dorthea urged the horse forward once again.

As they drove farther and farther from Waco, the two women discussed the big event planned for this afternoon.

Traesa hoped she hadn't made a mistake agreeing with Dorthea. She didn't want anything to give Wilson a reason to be angry with her. Their relationship had been progressing so well lately, and she wanted it to continue that way.

"Turn around, Dorthea. I want to go back to Waco." Her heartbeat sounded strong in her ears.

"I know you'll enjoy it when we get there." Dorthea smiled at her. "I've heard a lot about it, and I want to see it for myself." She turned her eyes back on the road as she drove along. "There are lots of families who came early and are living in tents. There's even a Ringling Circus tent where people are being fed." Excitement rang in her voice.

"You don't understand." Traesa had to convince Dorthea to take her back before Wilson found out where they were. "My husband told me not to go."

"This is 1896. Women don't have to be dominated by men. My brother told me not to go too. But I'm older than he is, and I don't have to obey him." She was almost shouting over the sound of the fast hoofbeats.

What does that have to do with anything? "I thought you were twins."

Dorthea turned toward her again. "I was born a few minutes before him."

"A husband telling his wife not to go is far different from a brother telling his sister."

Traesa wished the girl would keep her eyes on the road, because the carriage veered a little as it bounced along. She clutched the seat so she wouldn't be thrown out.

"We're over halfway there. If I turn around now to take you back, I'll miss seeing it, too."

Traesa hadn't thought of that. Why had she agreed in the first place? She didn't want to be the reason Dorthea missed the event. There wasn't anything Traesa could do now but just go along with her. Maybe it would be worth the trip. She tried to relax but couldn't.

~

*W*ilson leaned back in the chair he pulled up beside Theodore as they pored over the legal documents they had created for Theodore's client. Everything was in order. Their work was finished.

"Thank you, Wilson. I never could have gotten this done so quickly, if at all." Theodore heaved a sigh of relief. "I owe you so much more than the price we agreed on."

"We made an honest deal. Remember, you've paid our expenses too."

They gathered up the documents and made sure they were in the correct order.

"Traesa will be surprised we're finished this early. She's spending the day with Dorthea."

Theodore unlocked one of the new-fangled metal file cabinets and placed the files in a hanging file folder. Too bad Mr. Harrison hadn't gotten that kind of cabinets for their files. When he got back to Fort Worth, he planned to talk to Carl about acquiring some for their office. Since they had been alphabetizing the files as they searched, it would be easy to put the documents in the cabinets in order.

Theodore turned toward him. "Why don't you come home with me? Maybe Dorthea and Traesa would like to go eat at the hotel for supper."

"That sounds good to me."

When they arrived, the women weren't there. Theodore went to talk to their housekeeper. He came back with a frown on his face. "I have a bad feeling. The women left in the carriage quite a while ago, and they haven't come back. The housekeeper said they headed toward the river. I'm afraid they went to see the train wreck."

Anger almost choked Wilson. Why would Traesa do such a hair-brained thing? She could be in danger. After all the time he'd spent protecting her, this was her way to thank him. Going against his warnings.

"I'm sorry about that."

"I told Traesa not to go out there." Wilson couldn't keep the anger out of his voice.

"I'm sure it was Dorthea's idea. I told her not to go too. But that woman is obstinate."

"Maybe we're wrong." At least he hoped they were. "Perhaps they'll soon be here."

"What should we do?"

Wilson couldn't ignore the fear he felt. "Why don't you stay here, in case they come home? I'll borrow one of your horses and ride out to the wreck. I hope I can get there by four o'clock when the wreck is supposed to take place. If they aren't there, I'll come straight back."

"That sounds like a good plan." Theodore dropped onto the sofa and leaned his head back.

There wasn't much traffic on the road. He didn't like to ride a horse too hard, but today they galloped. It was too close to four o'clock for comfort when he left. He would never make it by then. He would have to hold on to his temper because he didn't want to scare Traesa again. He felt like shouting at her and dressing her down. *Lord help me.*

Every minute that passed felt like an eternity. He imagined all kinds of scenarios where she would be injured or even killed. Just when they were making headway toward a better relationship.

He reached the last hill at the edge of the valley right before five. He hadn't heard an explosion. Maybe the engineers were right. Just as his head topped the hill, the trains hit head-on. The sounds of metal against metal echoed across the valley. He could see the engines. One bucked up and came down hard on the other, and a giant explosion spewed steam and red-hot metal bits high into the air.

His horse emitted a sound more like a scream than a neigh, bucked once, then crowhopped. Wilson gripped the reins tighter in his hands so he wouldn't fall off. With all the noise, he leaned forward, so his mount could hear his soothing words. It took longer than he thought it would to completely calm the horse.

His gaze hurried around the area.

He saw the women's carriage farther down the ridge with the reins tied to a tree. *They are here.* Their horse was fighting against the reins, trying to get away from the ear-splitting clamor. He rode over to the same tree. After jumping off, he tied his horse to the trunk of the same tree, then tried to calm the other animal. As soon as it was under control, he turned back to look at the chaos below.

His heart ached to get to Traesa. What if she was injured or even dead? Why hadn't he realized before today that he loved her? Completely. Now he might have lost her before he ever got the chance to tell her. His anger drained away, replaced by anguish.

People were lying on the ground, others trying to help them as burning hot pieces of metal of many sizes lay scattered all around. A grandstand had been too close to the tracks. Debris had torn through the wood. He wondered if anyone from that platform was hurt.

He tried to remember what Traesa wore today. He could look for the hat she usually wore with the dress, but he was too upset by what was happening around him to recall.

210

As he walked carefully through the field of debris, he felt as if he were in a war zone. Cries of agony rang out accompanied by a cacophony of people crying out the names of loved ones they were searching for. A man stumbled by holding a hand over one eye. Blood trickled between his fingers. Then Wilson noticed another man, who had passed out. He hunkered beside him to see if he could help, but found that the man was deceased.

He had to find Traesa. He stood up and scanned the field, turning slowly in a circle. For too long, he saw neither Traesa nor Dorthea. If anything happened to Dorthea, Theodore would be devastated, too.

Many people were helping the wounded. Others wandered around as if in a daze. There in the midst, he spied Traesa holding a small child in her arms, her red hair radiant in the bright sunlight. She seemed to be trying to help.

He ran toward her. "Traesa!"

She turned and looked at him, and fear lit her eyes. He regretted that his previous anger had put it there.

A woman took the child from her and held it close.

He reached his wife and gathered her in his arms. "Oh, my darling, I love you so much."

Her tear-filled eyes widened and her lips trembled as if she was about to cry.

He wiped the tears from her cheeks. "To think I might have lost you without ever telling you that." His lips descended to hers, then gently caressed them.

Never had he imagined something so sweet, so soft. He felt their hearts entwine. As she participated in the kiss, he felt a fusion of their emotions. Their first step to becoming one flesh.

When Traesa had heard Wilson's voice, she regretted not making Dorthea stop and let her out of the carriage. She could have walked back to Waco, no matter how long it would have taken her. She never wanted to disappoint her husband. Even when he reached her and pulled her into his arms, she still expected him to lose his temper. And she wouldn't blame him.

As she heard the words, "I love you," her heartbeat accelerated. She'd loved him for quite a while. Even though he had been treating her well, she never realized he might love her.

Their kiss connected her heart to his with a strength that could not be broken. They were truly married in every way but one. And now she was ready to take that last step. Their love for each other would carry them through all the things they would have to face in their life together.

She didn't even think about the throng of people surrounding them until the kiss ended. She glanced around and noticed no one was paying attention to them.

She said, "We need to find Dorthea."

Her husband nodded. "There are plenty people taking care of those who are injured. I see a few doctors with their medical bags. We need to get back to Waco. Theodore is waiting at home in case you and Dorthea came there before I got back."

Within a few minutes, the three of them climbed the hill to the tree where the horses were tied. Wilson helped the two women into the back seat of the carriage.

"I'll tie my horse behind and drive you back to town."

～

After dropping Dorthea and the horse at home, Wilson and Traesa headed to the hotel to rest a little then get ready to have supper with Theodore and Dorthea in the restaurant there.

Wilson picked Traesa up from the carriage seat by lifting her with both hands on her waist. The imprint of the heat lingered after her feet were on the ground. His touch released a flock of hummingbirds in her stomach.

As they entered the hotel, Wilson was surprised to see Carl waiting for them. "What are you doing here?"

"I need to talk to you…privately." He looked nervous.

Wilson wondered what he had on his mind. "Do you want to see just me, or do you want Traesa to join us."

"Traesa should be there too."

"Do we need to go up to our suite?" With all the people milling around, Wilson didn't consider the lobby of the hotel private.

Carl nodded and followed them as they headed up the stairs.

When they were seated in the parlor, Wilson said, "I'm not sorry to see you, but I can't help but wonder what is so important that you rode the train down here."

"Two things, actually." Carl lifted the Gladstone bag he had been carrying into his lap and pulled out two files. "First, my wife came and stayed several days. She doesn't want to live in Texas. She wants us to go back home. So according to my uncle's will, I must offer you the opportunity to buy the practice. Are you interested?"

Wilson looked at Traesa. "What do you think?"

She gazed at him for a few moments while the men awaited her reply. "Wilson, whatever you want is fine with me."

"I have a lot of years invested in the firm, so yes I'm interested."

Carl opened one of the files. "I have drawn up a contract that I think is fair to both of us. It will allow you to pay for the practice over a two-year period. If you agree, we can sign it now."

He handed the form to Wilson. He read every page carefully. "You're not charging a lot."

"My uncle left me other money and investments as well as his house, enough to take care of our family for several years. I'm fine with the contract amount."

"Okay. I'll sign it." After he finished, he handed both copies to Carl to sign. "I can write you a check when we get to Fort Worth."

"My wife and I will be leaving for Iowa tomorrow when I arrive back in Fort Worth. You can mail one to me, if you need to."

"Traesa and I will be on tomorrow's train as well. We can take care of it before you leave."

Carl opened the other file. "I think I've found what you've been looking for." He handed two documents to Wilson.

Wilson's heart leapt when he saw what they were. One was the adoption of Traesa by her grandmother. That made her equal with her Hilliard father and mother, not Quinton and his sisters. That explained why the other adoption papers hadn't been signed. Her grandmother had decided to adopt her instead.

The second document was the final will of her grandmother that made Traesa the main heir. All the properties were hers, and half the monies. The other half were designated. Some to each of their employees, then savings accounts for Alice and Clara, with money going to them each month until they marry with the rest going to each couple on their wedding day. A smaller savings account had been established for Quinton should he ever mend his ways and return home clean and sober. She also included an account for Charlotte even though her Duke was quite wealthy. This sounded more like the Mrs. Hilliard he had grown to love while he cared for her holdings.

Wilson stood and Carl joined him. "These are exactly what I

wanted to find. I'll share them with Traesa and her family when we get back to Fort Worth."

~

*T*raesa wondered what the papers said, but she could wait until they got home. Her mind was on what had happened in her marriage earlier that afternoon.

She accompanied her husband and Carl to the dining room where they found the Collins twins waiting at a table set for five.

Wilson introduced the Collins twins to Carl, and they all got acquainted.

After they ordered their meal, Theodore glanced at his sister. "What happened out there today?"

"I got there just in time to see the explosion." Wilson grimaced. "Why was the train wreck so late?"

Traesa looked at Dorthea. "Do you want to tell them?"

"No, you go ahead."

Wilson stared at each of them in turn. "Somebody tell us."

Traesa couldn't keep her thoughts off the kiss, but she went ahead. "At four o'clock, trains were still arriving full of people who wanted to see the wreck, so they waited until the last train arrived."

They continued discussing all the excitement until their food arrived.

Traesa was looking forward to being alone with her husband. She was so excited she couldn't eat much.

When they left the dining room, Carl registered for a room in the hotel. They could go with him to the depot tomorrow.

Wilson put his arm around her waist as they climbed the stairs. The flight of the hummingbirds sped up. Once inside the room, he again pulled her into his tight embrace. He dropped gentle kisses on each eyelid. Then down her cheeks until he reached her lips. By that time, she was eager for more. His gentle kisses turned passionate. She had read about passion in books but never understood the power of that word until this moment.

Tonight, they would consummate their marriage. What a blessed event that would be.

Dear Readers,

Thank you for choosing to read *A Heart's Forever Home.* I hope you enjoyed Wilson and Traesa's story as much as I enjoyed writing it.

If you'd like to know what happens next in their lives, I'm writing an Epilogue. Email me: safe-LDwrites@flash.net to request a copy of the epilogue. Let me know if I can add you to my newsletter subscription list as well.

I have always been careful when writing historical novels to make every thing in the book authentic to the time period, because I want readers to have the correct picture in their minds.

I'm now making sure I have actual historical events as part of my story. With Wilson and Traesa, the orphan train is one of these events. One of the trains from New York City had Fort Worth, Texas, as the final stop before returning.

The Orphan Train Movement was a program that transported children from crowded Eastern cities of the United States homes in other states. The orphan trains operated between 1854 and 1929, relocating about 250,000 children. According to the Star-Telegram (https://hometownbyhandlebar.com/?p=30087), in 1887 Fort Worth's first orphan train arrived. When it arrived in Fort Worth in 1887, not all the children were claimed by prearranged adoptive parents. Isaac Zachary Taylor Morris and his wife Belle took in the unclaimed children to find homes for them. This led eventually to the creation of the Edna Gladney Orphan's Home.

The major event that was a catalyst to Wilson realizing he had fallen in love with his wife actually happened. The Crash at Crush. For more information, here's one link: https://en.wikipedia.org/wiki/Crash_at_Crush. You can also find other links as well.

Dr. Pepper was created at the Old Corner Drug Store in Waco, Texas.

Mineral Wells, Texas, was mentioned near the end of the book. You can learn more about that town and it's "Crazy Water" in the next book, *A Heart's Redemption.*

Lena

While researching the hotels in New York City in 1896, I chose the Waldorf. That was before there was a Waldorf Astoria hotel. In the information, I found this information about how the Waldorf Salad came to be. The recipe is different from any Waldorf salad I'd ever eaten. I thought you readers might like to try it.

Mr. Oscar Tschirky, the *Maître d'hôtel,* a Swiss immigrant who became known as "Oscar of the Waldorf," is credited with creating this salad in 1893, a timeless dish whose popularity has spread far past the Waldorf's exclusive doors. Over time, various things have been added by other cooks. And I've never seen one that contains the lettuce.

~

ORIGINAL WALDORF SALAD

1 medium ripe apple
1 stalk celery, chopped
¼ cup mayonnaise
 Salt and pepper
2 cups lettuce, torn into bite-size pieces

Peel apple and cut into halves. Remove core and slice halves 1/4-inch thick. Reserve 4 slices. Cut remaining slices into thin strips.

In a medium bowl, mix celery, mayonnaise and apple strips; season with salt and pepper to taste. Arrange on lettuce and top with apple slices.

Did you enjoy this book? We hope so!
Would you take a quick minute to leave a review where you purchased the book?
It doesn't have to be long. Just a sentence or two telling what you liked about the story!

Receive a FREE ebook and get updates when new Wild Heart books release: https://wildheartbooks.org/newsletter

Don't miss *A Heart's Redemption*, book 4 in the Love's Road Home series!

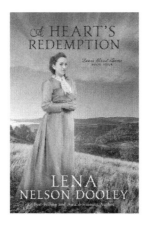

Chapter 1

OKLAHOMA
SUMMER 1899

The JJ Ranch couldn't afford to lose any more cattle.

Dave Jefferson rode along the fence line, searching for the break where stock had escaped from the pasture. The herd was still recovering from the terrible storm in February, which blew a swath of ice and snow down the central part of the United States from the Canadian border all the way to Mexico. Ranchers caught in the path lost an enormous number of cattle in the unheard-of occurrence. According to the *Fort Worth Gazette*, even southern-most points like the Rio Grand Valley and Galveston Bay froze over.

Every animal he could find mattered if the ranch was going

to recuperate. The new calves born since the storm had increased the herd, but not to pre-storm numbers.

Hoof beats in the far distance interrupted his thoughts. Who could be out here riding that hard? Very soon, a rider appeared on the horizon, headed straight toward Dave.

What was Bart doing riding his horse hell bent for leather? He usually treated Scout with the utmost care. Something must have happened, and it had to be an emergency.

Dave headed toward the foreman, meeting him halfway.

Bart dismounted. "You gotta come back to the ranch house right away."

Dave's heart beat double-time. "What's wrong? Has something happened to the boss?" The man had been under the weather a lot lately.

Bart looked down and scuffed the toe of his boot in a patch of dirt. "He don't look so good. He's been in bed most of the day, and his lawyer and the doctor are with him right now."

Doctor? Lawyer? Without waiting for another word, Dave rode Smoky just as fast as Bart did Scout. *Please, Lord, don't let me be too late.*

Jericho Johnson had changed his life over ten years ago. Dave wasn't ready to lose the older man now. He still had a lot to learn from him.

When he reached the ranch headquarters, he went straight to the house. He burst through the front door and ran down the hallway to Jericho's bedroom, Bart not far behind.

Dave stared at his mentor lying in the bed, his face white as the pillowcase where his head rested. Even the faded gray hair seemed to meld with the bed linens.

"Yer here, son." Jericho's voiced rasped through the room.

Dave knelt beside the bed. "How're you feeling?"

The older man's gaze shot toward the lawyer, then the doctor.

That scared Dave even more. "What's going on here?" He couldn't bring himself to face the obvious. Jericho wasn't going to make it this time.

He'd never cried in front of anyone, not even during the beatings he sustained from his stepfather. Today, tears dripped down his face, because the man before him was more of a father than any other had been.

Jericho gave a slight nod toward the other two men in the room. "Listen to them right now." The old man's eyes drifted shut.

Dave stood, grabbed his bandana from his hip pocket, and wiped his tears away before turning to face them. "What's he talking about?"

The doctor looked troubled. "You know how Jericho has been getting weaker and weaker."

Both Dave and Bart nodded.

"His heart trouble is getting serious."

"Heart trouble?" Dave gazed back at his mentor. "How long has he had heart trouble?"

The man wasn't moving at all.

The doctor shifted his position and stared straight at Dave. "Quite a while. He didn't want me to tell any of you. Then this morning, one of the cowboys came to town and asked the two of us to come back with him."

Who had gone and why didn't the cowboy didn't let Bart and him know?

"I've done everything I can for him." The doctor's voice hung with sadness.

"So why is the lawyer here?" Evidently Bart was just as disturbed by what was going on as he was.

"He wanted to change his will." The lawyer held up a short stack of papers. "We finished just before we sent for the foreman and you."

The strength slipped from his limbs. The man who'd been a mainstay for him wasn't going to make it. He felt hollow inside. What would happen to the ranch? Where could he go?

The doctor walked by him toward the head of the bed. He leaned over Jericho and felt for a pulse, then stood up. "You men got here just in time. He was holding on the best he could until after you came. Now he's gone and out of his misery. He asked me to tell you not to worry about him. He was going home."

That sounded like Jericho. He often talked about life being fleeting and that he would go home to be with Jesus. Today was that day, but much too soon for Dave. After what his mentor had taught him about the Lord, he would have to deal with his loss like a man of God. That was the greatest gift Jericho had given him. An introduction to Jesus.

"Bart and Dave, please come with me." The lawyer motioned for them, and Dave fell into step behind him as he led them to the ranch office. He wasn't ready for official details, not when his dearest friend lay lifeless in the other room.

When they were all inside, the lawyer closed the door and moved behind the desk to sit in Jericho's chair. After laying the papers in order, he gestured for them to sit in the chairs across from him.

"Jericho insisted that I have the reading of his will as soon as he passed on."

Dave glanced at Bart. The foreman looked as distressed as he felt.

The lawyer cleared his throat. "I know this is a lot to take in right now. Jericho had told me often about how close the three of you were. About the Bible studies and the changes you made in your lives. He was very proud of you, and he loved you like the sons he never had."

That sounded odd to Dave. He was thirty-eight years old, and Bart was near sixty. Since Jericho was in his seventies, the timeline for children was way off. *Why am I thinking about this right now?* Because he didn't want to think about the dead man in the other room.

The lawyer picked up the first page. "He wrote a letter to each of you. I'll give you a copy after the reading. I'll also give each of you a copy of the will. I'm only going to tell you the high points of the document."

Dave leaned back in the chair and crossed one ankle over the other knee. He tried to clear his mind so he'd understand what the man said.

"Since Jericho Johnson didn't have any relatives left alive, he bequeathed all his possessions to the two of you. You will be co-owners of everything. He did make a provision that if you don't want to own the ranch together, each of you will have enough money to buy the other one out."

Bart stared at the lawyer, then at Dave, clearly as thunder-struck as Dave was. That was a lot to take in all at once.

After going through a few more details, the lawyer stood and handed a sheaf of papers to each man. "Jericho insisted that his funeral and burying be the day after he died. The doctor is making sure his body gets to town, and he'll contact the reverend. We'll see you tomorrow at the church."

He shook each man's hand and left the room.

Dave and Bart just stared at each other. The tears in Bart's eyes matched the ones collecting in Dave's.

Dave rode alongside Bart to town the next day. They wore their Sunday best clothes, and silence accompanied them. Too many thoughts swam in his mind of just how much Jericho Johnson had meant to him. How much he'd learned about ranching from the man, as well as all the spiritual lessons he'd experienced.

As they approached the church, he was surprised to see so many buggies and individual horses clustered around the white clapboard building. Word must have spread fast for this many people to be at the funeral. Of course, Jericho had been loved by nearby ranchers and townspeople alike.

Someone had already dug the grave in the cemetery not far from the building. The slash in the ground matched the hole in his heart.

The service was short, but meaningful. The pastor had asked five people to share about Jericho. Dave was thankful he hadn't been one of them. He wasn't sure he could get through talking about his beloved mentor without weeping.

When they finished lowering the casket into the ground, all the men helped shovel the dirt to fill the hole. That was just Jericho's earthly body. Now he was in heaven, and Dave couldn't wish him back here. He was only grieving for his own loss. He knew Jericho was rejoicing with Jesus.

Afterward, most everyone went to the schoolhouse for the funeral meal. Dave hung back until they were all gone.

He stood a moment before he spoke, gathering the words that had been pressing in his chest. "Jericho, I'll miss you to my dying day. I've tried so hard to make the restitution you taught me about, and I've found every single person, except one. I won't quit looking, but I've run out of ideas about how to find her. I vow not to give up this quest though. No matter how long it takes me."

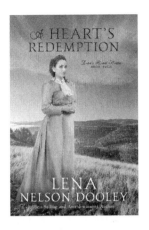

GET *A HEART'S REDEMPTION* AT YOUR FAVORITE RETAILER.

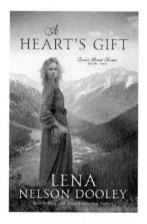

Book 1: A Heart's Gift

Book 2: A Heart's Forgiveness

Book 3: A Heart's Forever Home

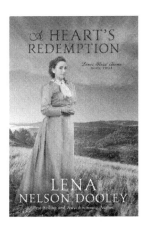

Book 4: A Heart's Redemption

ABOUT THE AUTHOR

Multi-published, award-winning author Lena Nelson Dooley has had more than 950,000 copies of her 50+ books sold. Her books have appeared on the CBA and ECPA bestseller lists, as well as Amazon bestseller lists. She is a member of American Christian Fiction Writers and the local chapter, ACFW - DFW. She's a member of Christian Authors' Network, and Gateway Church in Southlake, Texas.

Her 2010 release, *Love Finds You in Golden, New Mexico*, won the 2011 Will Rogers Medallion Award for excellence in publishing Western Fiction. Her next series, *McKenna's Daughters: Maggie's Journey* appeared on a reviewers' Top Ten Books of 2011 list. It also won the 2012 Selah award for Historical Novel. The second, *Mary's Blessing*, was a Selah Award finalist for Romance novel. *Catherine's Pursuit* released in 2013. It was the winner of the NTRWA Carolyn Reader's Choice contest, took second place in the CAN Golden Scroll Novel of the Year award, and won the Will Rogers Medallion bronze medallion. Her blog, A Christian Writer's World, received the Readers' Choice Blog of the Year Award from the Book Club Network. She also has won three Carol Award Silver pins. In 2015 and 2016, these novella collections—*A Texas Christmas, Love Is Patient,* and *Mountain Christmas Brides* have all appeared on the ECPA bestseller list, one of the top two bestseller lists for Christian books.

She has experience in screenwriting, acting, directing, and voice-overs. She is on the Board of Directors for Higher Ground Films and is one of the screenwriters for their upcoming film Abducted to Kill. She has been featured in articles in Christian Retailing, ACFW Journal, Charisma Magazine, and Christian Fiction Online Magazine. Her article in CFOM was the cover story.

In addition to her writing, Lena is a frequent speaker at women's groups, writers groups, and at both regional and national conferences. She has spoken in six states and internationally. The Lena Nelson Dooley Show is on the Along Came A Writer Blogtalk network.

Lena has an active web presence on Facebook, Twitter, Goodreads, Linkedin and with her internationally connected blog where she interviews other authors and promotes their books. Her blog has a reach of over 55,000.

- Website: https://lenanelsondooley.com
- Blog: http://lenanelsondooley.blogspot.com
- Blogtalk Radio: https://blogtalkradio.com/alongcameawriter/2

facebook.com/Lena-Nelson-Dooley-42960748768

instagram.com/lenanelsondooley

pinterest.com/lenandooley

goodreads.com/lenanelsondooley

twitter.com/lenandooley

amazon.com/author/lenadooley

linkedin.com/in/lenanelsondooley

ALSO BY LENA NELSON DOOLEY

The McKenna's Daughters Series:

Maggie's Journey: Near her eighteenth birthday, Margaret Lenora Caine finds a chest hidden in the attic containing proof that she's adopted. The spoiled daughter of wealthy merchants in Seattle, she feels betrayed by her real parents and by the ones who raised her. But mystery surrounds her new discovery, and when Maggie uncovers another family secret, she loses all sense of identity. Leaving her home in Seattle, Washington, Maggie strikes out to find her destiny. Will Charles Stanton, who's been in love with her for years, be able to help her discover who she really is?

Mary's Blessing: When her mother dies, Mary Lenora must grow up quickly to take care of her brothers and sisters. Can love help her to shoulder the burden? Mary Lenora Caine knows she is adopted. As she was growing up, her mother called her "God's blessing." But now that she's gone, Mary no longer feels like any kind of blessing. Her father, in his grief, has cut himself off from the family, leaving the running of the home entirely in Mary's hands. As she nears her eighteenth birthday, Mary can't see anything in her future but drudgery. Then her childhood friend Daniel begins to court her, promising her a life of riches and ease. But her fairy-tale dreams turn to dust when her family becomes too much for Daniel, and he abandons her in her time of deepest need. Will Daniel come to grips with God's plan for him? And if he does return, can Mary trust that this time he will really follow through?

Catherine's Pursuit: In book three of the McKenna's Daughters series, Catherine McKenna begins a journey to find her lost sisters that turns into a spiritual journey for the entire McKenna family.

Lena's work is also featured in the following recent collections: *8 Weddings and a Miracle Romance Collection, A Texas Christmas: Six Romances from the Historic Lone Star State Herald the Season of Love, Warm Mulled Kisses: A Collection of 10 Christian Christmas Novellas, and April Love: A Collection of 10 Christian April Fool's Novellas.*

WANT MORE?

If you love historical romance, check out our other Wild Heart books!

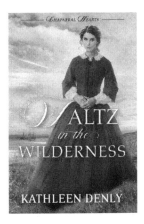

Waltz in the Wilderness by Kathleen Denly

She's desperate to find her missing father. His conscience demands he risk all to help.

Eliza Brooks is haunted by her role in her mother's death, so she'll do anything to find her missing pa—even if it means sneaking aboard a southbound ship. When those meant to protect her abandon and betray her instead, a family friend's unexpected assistance is a blessing she can't refuse.

Daniel Clarke came to California to make his fortune, and a stable job as a San Francisco carpenter has earned him more than most have scraped from the local goldfields. But it's been four years since he left Massachusetts and his fiancé is impatient for his return. Bound for home at last, Daniel Clarke finds his heart and plans challenged by a tenacious young woman with haunted eyes. Though every word he utters seems to offend her, he is determined to see her safely returned to her father. Even if that means risking his fragile engagement.

When disaster befalls them in the remote wilderness of the Southern California mountains, true feelings are revealed, and both must face heart-rending decisions. But how to decide when every choice before them leads to someone getting hurt?

～

Lone Star Ranger by Renae Brumbaugh Green

Elizabeth Covington will get her man.

And she has just a week to prove her brother isn't the murderer Texas Ranger Rett Smith accuses him of being. She'll show the good-looking lawman he's wrong, even if it means setting out on a risky race across Texas to catch the real killer.

Rett doesn't want to convict an innocent man. But he can't let the Boston beauty sway his senses to set a guilty man free. When Elizabeth follows him on a dangerous trek, the Ranger vows to keep her safe. But who will protect him from the woman whose conviction and courage leave him doubting everything—even his heart?

～

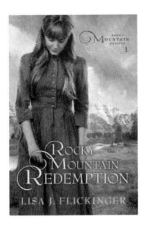

Rocky Mountain Redemption by Lisa J. Flickinger

A Rocky Mountain logging camp may be just the place to find herself.

To escape the devastation caused by the breaking of her wedding engagement, Isabelle Franklin joins her aunt in the Rocky Mountains to feed a camp of lumberjacks cutting on the slopes of Cougar Ridge. If only she could out run the lingering nightmares.

Charles Bailey, camp foreman and Stony Creek's itinerant pastor, develops a reputation to match his new nickname—Preach. However, an inner battle ensues when the details of his rough history threaten to overcome the beliefs of his young faith.

Amid the hazards of camp life, the unlikely friendship growing between the two surprises Isabelle. She's drawn to Preach's brute strength and gentle nature as he leads the ragtag crew toiling for Pollitt's Lumber. But when the ghosts from her past return to haunt her, the choices she will make change the course of her life forever— and that of the man she's come to love.

Made in the USA
Columbia, SC
24 September 2021